Other books by T. Linsay-Cole

Mendacity
Amends

Between Years
The Castaneda Witches
Death Movements: The Suicide Cult Phenomenon

Other Books by Howard-Hirsch Publishing

Body Mind Soul Money
The Mountain Woman's Wild Game Cookbook
Ooble Booble

The Mend

T. Linsay Cole

Howard-Hirsch Publishing

The Mend

An Epiphany Book

Published by Howard-Hirsch

Paperback edition published 2014
Reprint 2018

ISBN 978-0-9802307-3-4

Manufactured in the United States of America

Published simultaneously in Canada

Inside

"Inside each of us, there is the seed of both good and evil. It's a constant struggle as to which one will win. And one cannot exist without the other."

-Eric Burdon

Chapter One

"A very small degree of hope is sufficient
to cause the birth of love."
-Stendhal

The deep snow muffled the sound of slowed traffic and the high-pitched incoherence of kids quarreling over which stones to use as snowman eyes. Eric Rubin embraced the noise; it interrupted the silent hours he spent reading and made him feel connected to his neighborhood.

He walked along, shuffling his feet and kicking up little snowballs, his heavy boots crunching into smaller sets of footprints until a penny caught his eye and he bent to pick it up.

His fingers went right through it as he discovered that it was not a coin at all but a drop of blood that had been spilt recently enough to not have frozen. He looked ahead and saw more red drops smudged in the slush forming a clear path to a stone underpass. From within it he heard faintly echoed whimpering. It sounded like a wounded dog.

He already hated what he might find. He hated to see living things suffer. He had happened upon a wounded dog the previous summer, too late to save it.

The Mend

The howls of pain, as he rushed it to the veterinarian were less painful to his ears than being told that the hapless beast would have to be euthanized.

He kept the collar, in case he saw a missing poster, to help explain to the dog's worried family. Coincidentally, he had thrown the collar away just that morning.

He didn't run ahead. A wounded dog attacks when threatened. He walked with purpose toward the sound while taking off his tweed jacket in case he needed it to protect himself and to capture and transport the animal.

He noticed there were no paw prints in the snow, only woman-sized sneaker prints outlined in blood. He followed the blood and whimpers and began to run as he neared the tunnel.

"Somebody, please help me."

Under the stone pass, propped against the rough stones, shivered an emaciated, gray-faced young woman. Naked from the waist down, she held her wadded, bloody jeans with shaking hands.

She drew the long shallow breath of the exhausted, and despite the cold, she dripped with sweat. Black mascara tears covered her face.

As she noticed him she stopped calling for help and looked at him with relief.

The Mend

"Oh my God, you're hurt! Let me help you"
He feared she had been raped and steeled himself for the return of those that had done it, but they were alone and the girl didn't seem afraid, only spent.

He moved to wrap the jacket around the exposed teenager's waist, but she lifted her bloody clothes toward his face.

The rough denim fell away, exposing a still, blue newborn baby. Without a thought he wrapped the silk side of his jacket around the dead infant.

Just as she felt her baby's weight transfer to his hands the girl fell limp to the ground. He moved to catch her too, nearly dropping the almost weightless baby he had only begun to wrap.

Clumsily and quickly he clutched the baby to him, and he heard a soft popping sound like the cork from a bottle of champagne through a wall.

Immediately the infant wiggled to life as its mother lay suddenly still against the ice-frosted wall in the deep, muffling snow.

The tunnel had no such muffling effect. It amplified and echoed the sounds of the infant's gasping wail as Eric checked for an absent pulse on the teen whose face jolted him to a soul-tearing memory.

He remembered his wife and unborn son, he remembered his daughter, who would have been this girl's age, he felt the full power of his grief for the first time in years and his own sobs joined the new orphan's sorrowful song.

Chapter Two

"Cruelty, like every other vice, requires no motive
outside of itself; it only requires opportunity."
-George Eliot

"Bitch. What?!" Wayne Walters spat at his girlfriend
as she ripped her credit card statement from his hand.

Courtney, a skinny five feet tall, seemed bigger
with her fists flailing at her sides. She was electric
with rage. She held the paper up to his face. "I didn't
buy any of this shit and I sure didn't give you
permission to buy it." Her shaking hand rattled the
paper as she yanked it back from his attempt at
grabbing it. She stared at it. Her card was nearly at its
limit for the first time ever.

"We needed things. I can't get a job without
clothes and some of that, I bought for you!" Wayne
spoke defiantly.

"I already have a television, we didn't need more
wine, we sure as hell didn't need four cartons of
cigarettes, I don't even smoke. This was all for you."

"I'm not allowed to have anything I enjoy? You
buy that self-help crap all the time and I never

complain about that." Wayne turned his back to her and walked to the couch where he flopped on his side and reached for the remote. Before he could reach it, Courtney swiped it off the coffee table and it bounced across the floor.

"I *earned* that money Wayne and those CDs are an investment in my future."

"They're psychobabble sold to gullible people like YOU who never use them." Wayne laid back on the couch and watched Courtney pace.

She ignored the insult.

"What is this cash withdrawal for $300? That's a whole damned paycheck for me, Wayne." Her face was red with rage. "I want you out of here. You need to get a damned job and a place of your own and take care of your own damn self!"

Wayne sat up. "I don't have anywhere to go and it's just after Christmas. Nobody hires right after Christmas."

"Go to the Y or the bar. Maybe there's some other idiot out there with good credit you can take advantage of." Courtney sneered at the man she had not known long enough to hate.

Wayne slammed his beer bottle down on the table harder than he meant to. It shattered, cutting his hand and igniting his adrenaline.

Courtney laughed nervously a bit too loud.

6

Wayne impulsively picked up an empty bottle, threw it at her head and was surprised when it connected with a dull knock and coldcocked her. He had not meant to hit her, only to scare her.

Her expression went blank and her eyes closed slowly as she slumped to the floor still holding the credit card statement.

At least now she was quiet.

Wayne's mind worked quickly and savagely. He thought about tying her up until he could convince her to forgive him. He did not want to go back to jail.

He secured her where she could not escape until he had time to calm her down, then left to figure out his next move.

Courtney regained consciousness unaware of how much time had passed and realized she could neither move nor see. The smell of old meat, the cold and dead quiet was disorienting. She slowly realized as her brain began to function, that she was in her basement chest freezer. It didn't scare her until she tried to get out.

She attempted to adjust herself from the fetal position she had been forced into in order to fit into the cramped metal box and pushed against the rusty hinged door. It was locked. She banged on the sides with her palms, then louder with her knuckles.

The Mend

"This is not funny, Wayne. Let me out."

He did not reply.

"Right NOW! Wayne, let me out you fucker, it's cold in here!"

Stillness. No reply.

"Wayne, please! I'm sorry. You can stay, just please, let me OUT... I'm freezing to death... and there's not a lot of air in here! WAYNE!"

The silence made her heart race. He was not out there. She was alone. The hopelessness of her situation overwhelmed her and she began to cry, only stopping when she realized her sobs were costing her precious oxygen. She had read somewhere that people use less oxygen when they are asleep, so she closed her eyes and thought of her childhood bed at her grandparents' house. More than anything she wished she could wake up there and find that the last few days had just been a nightmare.

In a grocery store parking lot on the opposite side of Pittsburgh, Wayne had figured out a plan. He noticed that the store had too few witnesses inside to fit that plan. He would have to make them matter.

He chose a few strategic items, celebratory steaks, drinks and a balloon, and stood at the checkout of a bored, middle-aged cashier who seemed too dull to be able to remember his face. She would not be a good witness, but he had to try; the store was nearly empty. She didn't seem to be looking at any of the items she pulled across the scanner, and for a second Wayne worried that she might be blind.

She looked up long enough to see his helium balloon that read, "I love you" in neon letters across its shiny surface and tapped the price into the register.

A carton of cigarettes, two thick steaks and two bottles of cheap whiskey crept jerkily toward her on the stained conveyer belt.

He ducked and swayed, trying to make eye contact with the clerk. She didn't look up at him at all. People didn't forget his eyes. He needed her to see them.

"It's my turn to cook for my girlfriend." Wayne proclaimed to no one who was listening. "I'm so glad she's not a vegetarian."

The cashier glanced at the next item. Wayne was concerned, he had not gotten her attention. "I forgot a jar of mushrooms; do you mind if I just..." He waved his hands trying to get the attention of the concentrating clerk.

Without looking up, she reached into a basket of rejected goods beside her and scanned a package of mushrooms. She still had not seen his face. Wayne felt frustratingly invisible and that was not part of the plan.

With a not-too-subtle motion, he knocked one of the two bottles of whiskey off the belt. It shattered, splashing the jeans of the young couple that had walked up behind him with sticky brown liquid and shards of glass. A few other people passing looked in his direction. He smiled, feigning embarrassment. That had done it. He hoped the store's security cameras were recording.

"Got a bottle of *that* down there?" He smirked at the mildly-annoyed clerk.

"Clean up… and security at register three" She mumbled into the intercom. Wayne froze, that was not part of the plan either. He couldn't be delayed, he could not go back to jail.

"Look, I'm sorry, I'll pay for the whiskey, I've got to get going." He placed two twenties on the counter.

"Cancel security." the cashier droned into her microphone. Wayne took his haul, dropped a five-dollar tip onto the counter to insure he would not be forgotten, and grinned all the way to the car.

Courtney heard the freezer's motor kick on and felt new, warm tears running from her heavy closed eyes. It was all she felt, her legs had fallen asleep and her skin was numb. More than anything, she was tired. She rested against the crystalized steel wall of the freezer and sleep finally took over. A warm puddle beneath her and the smell of her own urine would be her last vague memory.

Upstairs, Wayne smiled and savored the last bite of his second steak with onions and sautéed mushrooms and took a long stinging drink of whiskey. Courtney was probably by dead now.

He hoped so, he couldn't see any other way to get out of charges for what he had already done. Assault, theft, kidnapping. If he let her out, she would press charges. He was not going to back to jail.

The house was wonderfully quiet. He scribbled on a paper tablet:

1. ~~Establish solid relationship...Grocery~~.

2~~. Time of death delay~~ ~~Freezer~~.

4. Proof of activity...Computer?

5. Create deniability...Witness to leaving.

6. Dump body...Club.

7. Establish alibi...Sister?

He took a photo of his empty plate with her phone, and typed "Yum, dinner was good to the last bite! Thank you, baby!" into the little dialog box on the screen. He tagged himself and clicked send.
Then he reached behind him, wiggled the mouse connected to Courtney's computer and felt something like divine luck was at play when the monitor flashed to life, she was still signed in. He wouldn't have to guess at her password. He always thought it would be something stupid like YOLO or LMFAO. (Sadly,

it was his name.)

He took her credit card from his wallet and downloaded two self-help programs using her open shopping account. He burned them to disks, wiped them, the phone and the credit card clean of prints, then he took one of the CDs to the freezer. Just out of curiosity, he held the shiny CD up to her nose to check for breath, and finding none, pressed it against her not-yet-frozen fingers to prove that after burning it, she had touched it. Then he took it to her car.

He whistled as he drove the car to her favorite club and walked home wearing a balaclava and black hoodie. He would not look unusual on the cold January night. Half way back and well out of range of any surveillance camera, he tucked the balaclava into his pocket and unzipped his pants to relieve himself on a tree. He took in a lungful of stinging air. He felt the hairs in his nose freeze as he inhaled his own whiskey-bar scented breath. It gave him an idea.

When he got back to Courtney's house he carefully picked up every shard of bottle glass from the kitchen, left the drops of his own blood on the table but scrubbed the small spot of her blood from the floor with a bleach-soaked dishcloth. He threw the rag and all the empty beer and whiskey bottles into a bag and took the trash to the curb just as the garbage truck arrived. He waved to the driver and smiled. Another witness to the seeming normalcy of the evening.

When the truck was out of sight he went back inside and found a video of Courtney and her friends laughing and talking at her sister's wedding.

They had attended the event together. He had gotten drunk and accidentally wiped his mouth on the bride's veil, which was inconveniently draped too close to his dinner napkin. When he realized what he had done, he tried to clean it off with in his water goblet not thinking that it was still attached to her head. He dunked her face into her soup and it was all caught on the wedding video that someone uploaded immediately. It went viral and Courtney's sister had not talked to him since.

He played the video and turned up the volume, it sounded like the women were in the kitchen.

Some kids playing late in the park across the street with their babysitter and he knew by the way they looked at the house that they heard it.

"Sounds like a party over there. You think they're having cake?" a kid wearing not enough layers said through shivering teeth. He rolled a snowball but didn't throw it. Instead he took a bite of it and let it melt in his mouth.

"Adults don't have cake at their parties." his

equally cold brother said. "That's pretty dumb huh? They just have beer. It's disgusting."

"You tasted beer?" The younger boy was impressed.

"Dad gave me a sip. It's gross." He threw his snowball at his brother, knocking his half-eaten snowball out of his hand.

"Stop lying, Alex, and get ready to go home, it's going to be dark soon." the kids' babysitter barked and looked up from her book. Her booklight was losing battery power and she noticed the boys shivering.

Wayne raised his last beer to his lips and watched the kids from the window while he carefully rummaged through Courtney's desk for anything of value.

He took three unopened box-sets of self-help CDs. Since they were new, he thought he might be able to trade them for food. He found a small handgun in the second drawer he didn't know Courtney had and pushed the items into a duffle bag along with vitamins and half a bottle of Oxycontin that Courtney had apparently been hiding from him as well with a nearly empty bag of pot in her nightstand.

He smoked the rest of a joint she had already rolled, then burned his to-do list and crushed the ashes in the ashtray with his lighter before walking to the basement.

In the same casual manner in which he had stuffed the items into the duffle bag, he stuffed Courtney's body into a large rolling suitcase, being careful to tuck her long red hair in as he zipped it. She almost didn't fit and he cursed as he bounced lightly on the bag to compress her stiffening body until he could fully zip it.

As soon as he saw the kids and their babysitter were about to leave, he took the loudly playing DVD out of the machine, wiped it clean and put it back on the shelf, turned off the TV and walked through the door slamming it behind him.

He took a long drag from the wilting helium balloon he had bought at the grocery store and yelled in his best feminine inflection, "Just get out, Wayne!"
He pushed as much air from his lungs as he could, took two fresh gulps of air and answered in his own voice.
"I will! I don't care, go back to the club with your new friends you little whore, I'm out. I'm not coming back this time."
He shoved the rolling suitcase into the back seat of his car, trying hard to make it seem light and threw the little bag with Courtney's valuables on the floor of the front seat, nearly burying it among a pile of empty fast-food bags and half-drunk soda bottles.

The car started roughly and he drove straight to the back entrance of the club, at the front of which he had left Courtney's car earlier.

After making sure there was no one around and that the security camera was still broken, dangling, facing the wall, he wedged Courtney's frozen body under an abandoned car that had been in the alley for weeks. He pulled her panties down several inches, laughing at his joke and drove away smoking the last of her menthol cigarettes.

Now he would have to do the most important part and it wouldn't be easy. He headed to her sister's house, hoping her new husband was home.

His luck held, and Jarrod Stone answered the door in sleep pants. Before Jarrod recognized him and thought to close the door, he squeezed his way into the house holding his cell phone against his head.

"Whatever you want, I'm done!" Wayne ended the call and threw his phone onto the couch he hoped to be sleeping on later. "She's nuts!"

He raised his eyes to see if Jarrod had bought the act and lowered his voice.

"Hey man, I appreciate you letting me in. There ain't no way in hell I can go back to my place with Courtney on the rag like she is right now. Can I just hang out here for tonight, or for a few hours until she calms down?"

The Mend

Jarrod glanced at his wife, who had been wearing a slinky teddy when he got up to answer the door but was now wrapped in his torn flannel robe. She scowled at him and disappeared back into the bedroom. He followed her and was back in just a few minutes.

"One night, Wayne, I mean it! In the morning, you go. My wife wants you to sleep in the garage but it's too damned cold. You can have the couch but you have to leave in the morning. Seriously." Jarrod's tone was stressed.

"No problem bro, I'm sorry, I will go in the morning. Courtney will cool down or she can be the one to move out." (It didn't sound like the calculated lie it was and Wayne was impressed with himself for the performance.)

A night with Courtney's family was the easiest way Wayne could create an airtight alibi. The end of the "argument" with his dead girlfriend had been loud, and convincing enough to Courtney's sister Kelsea, who shook her head in disgust as he collected his phone and put it back in his pocket.

He would be sleeping loudly as well; he intended to make some kind of noise all night. He wanted them to remember he was there, in excruciating detail.

As if anticipating the night ahead, Kelsea glared at her husband, as she walked through the small apartment now wearing a loose, fleece, keep-your hands-off-me nightgown and Jarrod glared at Wayne.

"One… One." Jarrod held up one calloused finger first to Wayne, and then to his unhappy wife.

Wayne realized that his night's lodging hinged on her good will and changed his tone.

"I appreciate this Kelsea, if it wasn't snowing so hard I would sleep in my car but it's beyond fucking freezing out there."

The snowstorm was the best part of the alibi. It kept Kelsea from going to reason with her sister and gave him the perfect way to make Courtney's death look accidental.

Although she had been dead for hours, the cold would make it appear as if it had just happened.

Kelsea and Jarrod, were the only people, outside of Courtney, that Wayne knew in Pittsburgh. He had been in town nearly nine months and had made no friends, on purpose.

Friends complicated things, so Wayne had learned to live without them. Courtney had been meant for a one-night stand as well but she had invited him to stay, he couldn't turn down the offer of free rent. Her sister and brother-in-law had been part of the package. The two girls were close. Although Courtney visited them often, Kelsea and Jarrod had left him alone for the most part, only inviting him for Christmas.

Kelsea threw herself on the chair facing the couch and tried to call her sister but the calls went straight to voice mail. Wayne explained that Courtney had probably turned off her phone after he had called her too many times.

She wanted to know why Courtney was so upset. He told them *he* was the one that was upset and they had argued when he found out she had gone out with a man she had met at work. He was very convincing when he said that despite the infidelity, he was willing to take her back.

He really had left several messages on her phone. It would make him seem less suspect in case they checked her phone later.

It was easy to fake her "calling" him to stage the angry phone call. He just changed his ring tone and 'answered' the preview sound. If there was one thing he had learned from his drunken father it was if you're going to need an alibi, details matter.

When she was found the next morning, he cried real tears (of desperation because her credit cards would be canceled). There was no one to pay the rent. He had nowhere to go but back to his half-sister's apartment in Cleveland.

He was sure he would not be welcome.

Two police cars were parked outside his sister's building when he got to Cleveland, three days later.

Wayne turned onto a side street and went the opposite direction. He was tired of being questioned.

The official cause of Courtney's death had been hypothermia and it had been ruled an accident. Even so, he was questioned. Jarrod and Kelsea had been questioned as well. The way Kelsea stared at him as he was answering the detective's questions, made him nervous but he answered every question perfectly. Nonetheless, the officers in front of his sister's apartment scared him. He wondered why the police would follow him to Ohio.

Maybe they had noticed that the call Kelsea and Jarrod had witnessed did not show up on Courtney's phone. No one had bothered to check *his* phone.

He should have been off the hook, he had been so careful, but the police in front of the building seemed to be waiting for him.

How did they even know about his half-sister? He had told no one about his only relative, or even that he was from Cleveland. Why were they there?

The Mend

If he had been confident enough of his defense to talk to the police, he would have found that they were not there for him, and that his sister was dead.

Inside the bleak, basement apartment, officers were looking for any indication of the identity of the father of the baby boy that had not been collected from the hospital the previous day. His mother had been brought in inside a coroner's van. Her license listed the address as the apartment they were now searching.

A matronly officer in her forties collected the only picture she could find, in a thin brass frame leaning against a chipped lamp. The photo was of a teenaged boy, a little girl and a woman who stood awkwardly close to one another but not touching on a beach. Despite the sunny day and their colorful clothing, no one was smiling. They all seemed afraid of the person taking the picture. The tortured smiles on their faces and long sleeves on their arms, when everyone else was wearing swimsuits, told the officer the family was probably covering signs of abuse.

She slipped the photo, along with a fake diamond cross necklace and a Bible signed, "To Wayne and Shelly Walters, Many Happy Years. -Reverend Davis." in a box that held only a few other items.

The Mend

The objects, with only sentimental value, would be the baby's only possessions; everything else would go to a Sheriff's auction to pay for his mother's cremation. They would not be enough.

Something told the officer not to keep a dog-eared letter from the girl's mother apologizing for her suicide and warning her daughter to be careful of her half- brother, "the shitting image of his father". The letter also implored her to think hard before having children. 'BAD BLOOD' was underlined and capitalized.

The officer crumpled the letter and dropped it into a trashcan that had already been searched. As a mother herself, she meant to protect the baby from that part of his past. With his troubled family gone, the infant could start his life with a new family, without a history.

Starting a new life was exactly what Wayne Walters wanted for himself. He liked to pretend he didn't have a family. His mother left when he was three and his father was a convicted felon who died of alcohol poisoning. His father had taught him two things, children were a burden, and nothing was illegal if you didn't get caught.

Years earlier his father had sideswiped a pregnant woman's car while in a drunken stupor, she was forced off the road and into a tree killing her instantly. Because the woman had been pregnant, he got a more extended prison sentence. Eight years.

Wayne Sr. started drinking the moment he was released and didn't stop until he was dead. He left Wayne Jr. with only the half-repaired clunker he had been driving, and a young stepmother far too sexy and submissive not to experience.

She killed herself soon after he seduced her, a month to the day after his father died, leaving him alone again with nothing but her daughter, who looked just like her and nothing like their father.

Loretta, his sixteen-year-old half-sister, had chosen to stay rather than go into the foster system. She could care for herself and had given him nothing but space, leaving for school early and going to extra-curricular activities or study sessions after school.

He drank away the small amount of money left in her mother's bank account while she avoided going home, sometimes sleeping over or staying until late with friends. Occasionally he found her asleep in the car.

One Saturday night when she thought he was out drinking, she accidentally walked in on him masturbating in her bedroom.

The Mend

The rage he had for his father, lust and grief for his stepmother, and a little too much alcohol and cocaine took control of his mind.

He raped his virgin sister, took his stepmother's wedding rings, the only thing of any value in the house, and left town that night. As far as he knew Loretta did not press charges, no one had come looking for him.

Now he found himself relieved that police presence had kept him away from her apartment. Recalling the memory of her pathetic face, so weak and broken and considering his rage at his present situation, seeing her again would have been dangerous at best.

He turned the car away from the building, oblivious to the existence of his newborn nephew struggling for his life half a mile away and started to make his way through empty streets to I-80. He knew the interstate ran all the way across the country: one road all the way to the West Coast.

That was the moment he made the decision to leave his old life behind and start a new one: a new life, with a new name.

It was just before he found the on-ramp that he happened upon the idea for his new identity. "Thomas" was the one legible word on a peeling cinder block wall of a condemned Italian restaurant.

That name and another partial word, "oni" were all that was left of a sign that once read: "Tony Thomas Pizza: Tony Pepperoni!"

He said the name aloud to try it out. "Thomas... Oni. Thomas Oni". It sounded uppity. He liked it.

He passed a silver BMW with New York plates and smirked at the blond, middle-aged lady driving beside him. She looked like funding for his trip.

"Hello, I'm Thomas." He whispered to her closed window. She noticed him, sped up a little and stared hard at the road ahead.

He looked around to make sure they were the only two on the street, then bumped his car against hers slamming it into an overpass abutment. She was knocked semi-conscious by the airbag.

He ran to the car, reached through the shattered passenger's side window and took her purse from the console beside her, He looked around again for witnesses, and considered taking her car but the damage was too heavy and it had a remote assistance service.

"Ma'am, do you need help?" the voice of the service was saying as walked back to his dented lump of a car and remorselessly drove around the corner to the highway on-ramp.

After ascertaining that he wasn't being followed, he took the cash, a cell phone, a Snickers bar and a bottle of Xanax from the purse, wiped it down and threw it out the window.

Then he yawned and slipped one of Courtney's CDs into the dusty CD player; the only part that worked of the broken factory radio in the dashboard.

"Congratulations on making a choice to change your life. You are listening to lesson one: *Speak Eloquently with Body Language*, this Disk One."

"Psycho-babble, but it beats this long fucking drive with nothing." He said to himself and repeated the name he had just given himself. "Thomas Oni. Hello, I'm Thomas Oni."

The car sputtered. He would only be able to use the woman's credit cards in Cleveland if he didn't want to be tracked. He made a mental note to also buy things he could sell along the way to fill his tank again.

"You are the architect of your future." the CD player droned to life as Thomas Oni was born in transit.

Chapter Three

"Once you start asking questions,
innocence is gone." -Mary Astor

Eric Rubin noticed his office door was open. He was sure he had locked it, so he clutched the heavy book he was holding with both hands and braced himself for an encounter with an intruder. A soft familiar humming voice inside soothed his nerves.

"Is this my mom?"

The little boy sat among carefully placed photos on the floor holding up a photo of a pretty young girl. The photos had been locked in a safe, which was in a locked closet, in his locked attic office.

"How in the world did you get to these pictures... and why?" Eric Rubin's calm hid his bewilderment and shock.

"I wanted to know why you never let me go upstairs so I came up here to find out."

"How did you get the doors and the safe open?"

"The door keys are on your car key ring. You always put the closet key on your bed stand every night and the combination is the numbers on the Catherine stone at the cemetery."

27

It made sense in a way that only Eric and the boy could understand.

He kept the decorative skeleton key his wife had custom-made for her Christmas closet around his neck, close to his heart to remind him of her.

His son, Zack, loved a puzzle. He never let a mystery go unsolved. The two had recently watched a television airing of The Goonies and once Zack realized that mysteries could mean treasure, he had gone on his own treasure hunt.

The numbers on Eric's daughter's gravestone would mean nothing to the bright five-year-old but they would stick in his photographic memory, becoming useful when faced with a set of numbers like the ones on the safe.

To the boy, the key on his chain looked like the key to a treasure box and the treasure was logically in the one room he was not allowed to enter on the third floor of the brownstone he shared with his adopted father.

"Is she my mom?"

"No Zack, but she should have... she could have been. She would have loved you so much." He scooped up the tiny 5-year-old with one arm and the keys with the other hand. "We will talk about this another time. It's time for you to go to your first day of school."

"I'd like to talk now please." the little boy's earnest and inquisitive nature was time-consuming. Eric knew he would have to answer more questions than he would have liked, but he knew that if he didn't answer the questions, they would keep coming until they were answered. He put Zack back on the floor.

"The girl in the photo is Catherine. She was my daughter. She died of leukemia, before you were born."

"I'm very sorry that I have no pictures of your mother. I didn't really know her." The one existing photo of his mother was buried unclaimed in the storage warehouse of the local police station. Eric resolved to put his own photos in an album to keep them from being neglected now that he could face looking at them again. He picked them up and stacked them in a drawer on his desk

"Your mom was an angel that breezed into my life, gave you to me and went back to heaven."

Zach picked up a pencil and rummaged through a nearby stack of papers for a blank page on which to draw.

"Angels are a myth. Heaven is also a myth, and myths aren't true. Are they?" This frank question was the result of an early vow Eric made to allow the child to discover religion organically. He was beginning to realize he had neglected his spiritual education. The boy had no concept of faith.

He did regard Zack's mother as an angel and he would continue to describe her that way. He wasn't sure how he would explain his opinion to his son. Opinions were not facts. The boy would insist on facts.

They had never spoken about the circumstances of his birth. How do you tell your son his mother was just an unfortunate stranger in a park? How could he understand that she died cold and terrified as a result of his poorly-timed birth?

Loretta Walters had come to Eric like a miracle at a time when he was loneliest. She had given him the gift of her only child, now *his* only child and the best part of his world.

The reality was that he could barely remember her face. When he had looked at her for those few minutes all he could see was the face of his Catherine. She would have been about the same age if she had survived.

In his time-worn memory, she looked like Catherine, but for the color of her eyes; a violet blue unlike any he had ever seen.
Now those eyes were staring at him in anticipation and wonder. Zack was waiting for Eric's reply.

He thought about the first time he held the child, both of them utterly alone in the world. He had not surrendered him to the police officers that had responded to his panicked call. They were not prepared for a newborn baby. They didn't even have a blanket.

Eric had held him against his skin like he had his own daughter… on the first worst night of his life… until the emergency responders were ready to examine him. They had to hand him back to collect the baby's unfortunate mother. Eric had insisted on going along in the quiet ambulance, keeping Zack tucked against him, warm and safe all the way to the hospital. His mother was taken to the morgue and the baby was taken to the newborn nursery on the delivery floor.

He remembered the sound of his cry as the caseworkers pulled him from his chest and walked away with him; it was strong, steady and mournful.

For three years, he visited the baby every week that his foster parents would allow. Eric could only observe as Zack was passed through several foster homes while the state searched for his unknown father. His uncommon DNA made the search difficult and eventually unresolved.

When no father could be found, he was finally placed for adoption, Eric was the first to apply, but his application was relegated to the bottom of a long list of people who wanted an infant boy.

As a beyond-middle-aged widower with no children, he was not the first choice for an adoptive parent. Healthy, normal, white, male babies were too easy to place.

But then Zack proved to be neither healthy nor normal. As an infant he cried night and day and began to fail developmental markers. He showed a tendency to react violently to the slightest touch. As a toddler he had multiple random outbursts, often in public. As a result, each prospective home failed to sign adoption papers after their ninety-day trial period. Some brought him back within a month.

With every home that gave him back, Eric came one step closer to adopting the pale, beautiful child.

Foster parents reported that only Eric could bring Zack out of his lengthy tantrums, so case workers eventually denied him visits, claiming he was too attached for the good of either. Eric had thought "too-attached" was an improper expression for the way he felt about the baby. He loved him from the moment he saw him. The separation nearly killed him. He couldn't eat nor sleep worrying about the toddler. Eventually the call came. He had reached the top of the list.

Zack was worth the wait. From their first day together, it was as if they had always been family. The moment the agency put the child into his arms, Zack took a long, loud sniff of his jacket, smiled and fell asleep. The tantrums were over.

The always-curious boy preferred the quiet, studious lifestyle of his new father to the constant stimulus of the foster homes, and Eric usually enjoyed answering his limitless questions. He was often stunned at the insight Zack provided in return. Sometimes he felt like he was speaking with his intellectual equal and the boy was only five.

There were no more lengthy tantrums and no more random behavior issues. Zack had become a sweet cooperative child in Eric's care.

He looked up at his dad as he finished a strikingly skilled and accurate drawing of Catherine from a photo that Eric had already gathered, along with the rest of the pile, and put away.

"Heaven and angels: myths, right?"

"We don't know if heaven is a myth for sure. Even teams of scholars can't agree. There is no hard evidence of heaven or angels, but that's the closest description I can give you for your mother. She was brave and beautiful."

Zack became quiet, stood as tall as he could and cleared his throat, a sign that his questions had been answered to his satisfaction...for now.

"Are we going to your school?"

"No little man, I'm retired. I don't have a school anymore. We are going to your school."

Eric didn't bother to lock the box, or the closet or the attic door on his way out. He knew it would be a waste of time. Now that the boy knew more about his past, he would have more questions. He didn't have the answers to the hard ones and he wondered if he had the strength to find them.

The soot-dusted brick building where Zack would be a kindergartner was foreboding even to Eric, but Zack seemed unfazed as he pulled his dad's hand, hurrying him into the building and out of the rain clouds that made him nervous.

Eric tripped up the stairs and bumped into a woman entering with her daughter.

"Oh, excuse me." He offered as he regained his balance and reached out to steady her. "I don't remember these stairs being this steep!"

"I remember them being taller." the woman replied with a forgiving smile. She noticed Zack.

"Is this your grandson's first day?"

"Son, and yes."

"I'm sorry, these days so many grandparents have to raise their grandchildren so I... but people are having families later." She looked at his face, expecting an explanation he wasn't going to give. Her smile-veiled look of pity sullied his happy situation.

He shook it off. "Not to worry," he smiled, "I'm sure I'm going to have to get used to that."

The woman's daughter suddenly broke free of her hand and snatched Zack's hand from Eric's. To his surprise, Zack didn't pull it away from her.

"You're the husband and I'm the wife." she said, "We are going shopping." She pulled Zack into the classroom and straight to the rows of toys other children were choosing from the disorganized shelves.

"You build the house, I'll get the baby!" the little brown-haired girl commanded.

"Wow, is he a cool kid." The woman mused as the two children fell into playing silently as if they had known each other all their lives. "Most kids hate it when she gets bossy like that! Let's go sign in while they are occupied."

She took his arm and pulled him to the line at the registration table.

Eric smiled. The bossy little girl was definitely following her mother's example.

The Mend

When the proper forms were finished, Eric turned, intending to wave good-bye, but Zack didn't look up. He was fixated on the blocks.

Eric noticed with dismay that Zack was building the walls of his little house in color patterns that looked like little houses.

A house made of houses. He wondered how long it would take for the teacher to confirm his suspicions.

It took two weeks. Zack was diagnosed as being in the high-performing autism spectrum.
The next twelve years would be a challenge for both of them. Eric, a former psychology professor set about designing a program to educate his son. The plan was for him to seem as normal as any other person. He succeeded in his quest… if "any other person" was a genius.

Chapter Four

"Doesn't the fight for survival also justify
swindle and theft? In self-defense, anything goes."
-Imelda Marcos

Wayne, now Thomas Oni, had been streamlining his
education over the years as well, beginning the day
after he left Cleveland.

The car's radio antenna was broken causing it to
only collect signals from radio stations less than five
miles away. Constantly changing stations was driving
Wayne crazy so he resorted to listening to Courtney's
psychobabble CDs. He enjoyed them more than he
thought he would and was soon listening to them with
great interest. He was eager to test out the exercises
that claimed to be able to give anyone the ability to
bend complete strangers to their will.

In a neighborhood gas station near South Bend
Indiana, he tried out his first trick from Disk 2 of *How
to Get Anything from Anyone* by tricking the cashier
at a highway gas station into giving him a free tank of
gas.

With a *smile and a hand touch*, he made the
nervous, obviously gay young clerk, believe that a

woman who had just pre-paid for her gas at pump 5 and gone to the bathroom had given him the wrong number.

He *confidently and urgently* told the young man that "his sister" was mistaken and he pointed to his own car at pump #7. The boy made the change and Thomas calmly filled his tank right up to the moment he saw the woman walking out of the store.

As he drove away, he laid heavily on the accelerator in his rush to get away and the old car sputtered and threatened to desert him to capture, perhaps in protest of the stolen gas, because he had smashed in its side panel or perhaps because Wayne had never once changed the oil in its engine.

He soon found that the gas station trick only worked when people didn't know each other. When he tried the trick near Joliet, Illinois he, more confidently and less urgently, claimed that a woman who had pre-paid for her gas was his wife.

The young girl behind the counter squinted in concentration and glanced up from counting the money in her drawer. "No sir, Mrs. Stocker is my history teacher, her husband, Mr. Stocker is my calculus teacher and he's over there, getting coffee."

This caused him to try the second trick (also from Disk 2), *Be Humble and Get Small*.

"Oh, my mistake, she's wearing the same jacket as my sister, I only saw her from behind…have you seen my sister? Maybe she went into the bathroom too."

He got small by bending down to re-tie his shoe and to let the few people waiting behind him check out and leave, including the oblivious Mr. And Mrs. Stocker.

For a few moments, he stood, checking his watch, acting as if he was waiting for a sister in the ladies' room, then he slipped out the door, followed closely by the eyes of the now slightly suspicious clerk who planned on using the lull in customers to put the bulk of the money in her drawer into a safe behind the counter.

He waved at her and gestured to the pile of clothes in his back seat, as if to say, "She's here and taking a nap!" an act for the camera too in case anyone was looking for him.

He drove his car around the block, changed into his black hoodie and put the balaclava over his head. Then he walked back to the store and robbed the girl just before she dropped the zippered bag of money she had been counting into the safe.

Just to be sure the girl would not connect the dots and report him to the police, he drove back to the store claiming to have forgotten to get a pack of cigarettes and a soda for his sister. He left just as the police were arriving.

The money got him as far as a small town outside of Salt Lake City where his car, empty and fed up with being an accomplice to his crimes, died of bad oil poisoning by the side of the road.

Wayne was not sorry to see it go. It was the last thing that connected him to his past. He was ready to be someone else, but first he would have to be someone in between.

Chapter Five

"Love is friendship that has caught fire. It is quiet
understanding, mutual confidence, sharing and
forgiving. It is loyalty through good and bad times. It
settles for less than perfection and makes allowances
for human weaknesses."
-Ann Landers

An old woman sat screaming in pain behind a barrier
of fallen cement blocks. Her leg appeared to be stuck
under some of them, Zack looked closer and noticed
that there was no blood. The woman was not stuck,
she only had one leg and the block over it was just in
front of it. He ignored her screams for help and
dodging debris from several explosions around him
ran in the opposite direction. There he found a silent
still infant holding a bottle of Coca Cola in its dead
hands. As he took it from the baby, a staircase opened
under the pram and he started down it. He looked
back and saw his best friend Noah Samuels
approaching the screaming lady. "No, man run!" he
cried out just as the woman pulled an automatic rifle
from a hole in the prosthetic leg lying beside her and
shot Noah dead.

"Damn! Dude, how did you know that screaming woman was a trap?" Noah's, brown eyes were wide with wonder as he pulled off his VR set and stared at Zack. "I've been burned by that part of the game 3 times by three different avatars. The last time that old woman was a trapped puppy. I thought there was no way to get out of that corner but you did it by taking a bottle from a baby… and this is your first time playing!" Noah blinked to confirm that what he saw was real, then squinted in suspicion. "Or did you just decide not to save her?"

"It's fairly obvious if you look at the overhead map at the beginning of the level. When you push through the blockage at the entrance, there is a fulcrum that triggers a falling wall. There are no life form readings in there, no supplies, no reason to enter…simple logic." Zack spoke as if it was something everyone should know and didn't look up from the game. "The baby was a doll, why would a doll be holding a soda, it had to be a key to another level."

"The overhead map is FIVE SCREEN BACK, nobody can remember what's five screens back, especially when they're seeing it for the first time." Noah didn't take his eyes off of Zack who had continued playing.

"Nobody?" Zack raised one eyebrow.

The boys were curled up on two of three banana-shaped gaming-chairs wearing headsets in front of a large flat screen television. Zack sat completely still, the only things moving were his fingers on the controller.

Noah reached out for the soda offered by their host, Jennifer Wilson. She had decided early on that the two gamers were far above her level and didn't want to embarrass herself by competing.

Hormone-riddled Noah couldn't help but stare at her butt as she turned to give a soda to Zack. Her hair smacked him in the face as she sensed his stare and snapped back around.

"Don't say nobody, you're playing against Nexesis90." She smiled down at her best friend, Zack, who blinked at the sound of the name but finished the level before removing his microphone to take a drink.

She had worn her cutest, snuggest jeans just for him, but he only had eyes for the game. She was disappointed that he didn't seem to notice, but she was used to it.

"Nexesis90? That's a computer, you can't beat it!" Noah exclaimed.

"Not a machine, mere man! This one."

Jennifer knew the compliment was lost on Zack. He took no pleasure in being the anonymous world champion of the online game. For him it was just a puzzle to solve.

"Is that true, Zack?" Noah looked like he had just met Jesus. "Are you Nexesis90?"

"I use a lot of names."

"Are you Berserker Void champion, Nexesis90?"

"That's one of my favorite games." Zack finally lifted his head and looked at Noah, noticing with dismay, the silent, awkward stare on his face.

His father had taught him not to draw attention to his talents. It had caused problems in the past.

Zack feared Noah's next step would be to announce online that he knew the identity of Nexesis90 and he knew that would ruin his carefully protected anonymity.

Zack's muscles suddenly appeared hard as stone and he sat frozen on the banana chair. He could not think of a way to correct the situation.

As if she read his mind, Jennifer regretted outing him and sang out, "Psyyyyyyyyche!!"

Noah looked disappointed and relieved at once.

"I just decided not to save her, man." Zack lied. "I wish I was as good as Nexesis90."

"Dude you're really good *too*, you should play against Nexesis90 sometime. That would be LIT!"

Zack still sat utterly motionless but slightly less rigid. Jennifer noticed. Noah, as usual, did not.

"No time to play anything now, we are late for prom committee. We have to decide on backgrounds and decorations." Jennifer clapped her hands loudly. "Up! Shoes! Let's be on time for a change!"

Jennifer hurried the boys out of the room, being careful not to actually touch Zack. She was fighting the instinct to hug him. She could see he was trying to calm himself after the near exposition of his freakish gaming talent. Instead of comforting her friend, she turned off the equipment and grabbed her car keys.

"I'm driving! She called out as if there was a choice. Neither Zack nor Noah had a license. Noah was self-conscious about it. He had used his Dad's car without permission and the old man had reported him. His license was suspended for a year.

Zack's father, having suffered a life-changing vehicular tragedy that he refused to speak of, couldn't bring himself to sign the papers. He wanted the boy to finish high school first. Eric Rubin was an unusually protective father, but not everyone knew why. Zack knew. He had researched. He didn't want to drive anyway. He liked to stay home.

Jennifer had gotten her license six months earlier out of necessity. Her mother worked full-time as a nurse, which often meant 18-hour shifts. More often than not she was unable to drive Jennifer to her piano lessons and dance classes. Eric Rubin gave her his wife's piano to practice on and paid for the lessons out of gratitude for her loyalty to his son. Zack built her a computer so that when she would have missed a lesson, her instructor could coach her online. Now that she was driving, she never missed a class.

Since the three friends had grown up together and lived on the same block, she drove Zack everywhere he wanted to go which was nearly nowhere. It was a perfect situation for her because she had a long-term crush on him and took every opportunity she found to spend time with him.

Zack was not a social creature. Rather than hanging out in the park or going out with friends, he loved nothing more than to use his daily screen-time allowance to demolish gaming opponents.

Jennifer saved her money for a gaming system, but when she mentioned that she was going to buy one, Zack built her one of those too. His screen time at home was limited, but at Jennifer's he could annihilate aliens, zombies and online competitors at will.

Jennifer had once remarked that she was glad he could keep his rage in the game. He was merciless while gaming but in his interactions in the physical world Zack didn't have a single cruel thought or action.

Noah did. His aggression was a result of his father's abusive alcoholism and his mother's absence. He and Zack met one morning after a night of failed attempts to protect himself from his father's drunken rage. His arms were badly bruised so he claimed he forgot his gym clothes in order to keep them covered with his long-sleeved t-shirt. Zack, oblivious to the obvious social clues, had offered to let him borrow his spare t-shirt and shorts. To save face, Noah had refused, claiming Zack smelled bad. Zack was always meticulously groomed and he pushed the issue asking classmates to smell his spare shirt, making Noah look like a fool. When the two were paired up in gym class later for one-on-one basketball. Noah floored Zack on his first approach and several thereafter. Zack left the gym with a number of bruises equal to Noah's, but not angry, only bewildered and determined to learn to play the game of basketball.

For weeks Noah felt guilty. He needled quiet Zack in the hallways hoping to provoke him to anger and allow him to punch him back for what he had done but Zack remained calm and kind. It wasn't until Noah discovered that Zack's best friend was Jennifer, the most desired girl in their school, that he apologized and they started building a friendship. Now the three were inseparable. Noah knew Zack was his only competition for Jennifer's attention, but he also knew that Zack was not interested in her like that, and that she also knew and loved him anyway. He respected their boundaries (most of the time).

Today he forgot all boundaries and punched Zack on the arm lightly as he ran past yelling, "I got shotgun!"

Zack visibly recoiled from the casual touch and stood trembling. His eyes were tightly closed and his head down. He was standing on the balls of his feet.

Jennifer made herself a visual block between Zack and Noah to protect him and called out, "Roll the windows down! It's hot in there!"

She hummed a song she had heard Eric hum when Zack needed help calming down and pretended to be looking for a different jacket.

Zack regained his composure and raised his head.

Jennifer gave him a warm smile, glad to be invited into his normal world again and they walked side by side matching step for step down the sidewalk to the waiting car.

Jennifer had accepted Zack as her responsibility from the first day of kindergarten and had never regretted it. Effortlessly popular herself, she carefully guided him through the many social pitfalls of life in public school.

She was pretty and smart, and thought of Zack's father as a suitable replacement for her own, who had died when she was an infant.

Because Jennifer liked him, and because when she shook her loosely curled tresses and blinked her blue eyes, girls imitated and boys were hypnotized, Zack had no trouble in school. But outside of her influence, his life was solitary and odd.

Zack read incessantly. He had devoured every book in his father's three-room library before he was in Jr. High and much of what he read, he committed to memory. He soon burned through every book in his small school, preferring reading to any physical activity.

Eric encouraged his son to join the drama club to use some of the knowledge he had collected. Because of his incredible memory and because he showed no sign of the self-consciousness that debilitated nearly every other pubescent boy in the class, he always got the most complicated roles. He had no idea that most people could not recite any script they had just read. It had almost exposed his oddness; a fatal social error for anyone in junior high school.

That year, at a Martin Luther King Day assembly, he innocently corrected a local celebrity who had been invited to read King's, "I Have a Dream" speech at the school. The insecure speaker considered the correction heckling, and to teach the upstart kid not to interrupt, he made the mistake of inviting him on stage to do a better job.

Zack recited the entire speech verbatim, complete with inflection and humbled the pompous speaker. The audience, completely silent during the presentation, jumped to their feet in a roaring standing ovation when he was done.

A teacher who knew of Zack's prowess at memorization, captured it on video and uploaded the speech. Local media edited the video and a clip aired that night to close out the evening news.

Eric spent the next day deflecting phone calls. He told them Zack had worked on the speech for weeks for a school project. In reality, he had seen it on television once when he was six.

Secretly, Eric worried that the child's biological father would see the broadcast and come for him, but he also knew that Zack's autism-related abilities had the potential to set him apart as a freak at the beginning of his adolescent years, and it wasn't what he wanted for the shy kid.

It was then that he taught Zack that using his intelligence conspicuously could lead to trouble.

That day as well, Jennifer valiantly became his impromptu manager. She was quick to notice his discomfort at the attention he was receiving and put herself between Zack and the small groups of kids that gathered whenever they saw him coming.

"Cool speech, Zack!"

"You should run for president."

"Step back and give the brainiac some breathing space." She rolled her eyes. "He's gotta study for the next assembly!"

She also scowled fiercely at the girls who for the first time noticed his violet blue eyes and smiled at him.

Zack never noticed the adoring looks from the girls, nor the jealous ones from the boys. He only felt comfortable in the presence of his father or Jennifer, and sometimes Noah, but the protective instincts of all three concealed that from the world. They taught him to spot a smile and return it, to reach out his hand when one was offered. People thought he was shy and sophisticated.

Eric knew that Zack absorbed every word he heard regardless of what else he was doing but he taught him to nod to show people he was listening. He also taught him to tone down his words to the level of the person to whom he was talking.

He never had to dumb down for Jen. She rose to his level. She studied to keep up with him, taking piano classes when he told her he loved concertos. She played intricate pieces to impress him and learned his favorites by paying attention to what was on the playlist on his phone. Technically, he played better than she did, but he loved the way she played so he never told her.

Eric warned Zack that one day when they went away to college, everything would change.

He did his best to diversify his son's interests, enrolling him in art classes, taking him on extended vacations, and giving him complex projects to complete.

Each time when the project exceeded expectations, or the classes became redundant, Zack would go straight back to Jennifer to share the experience, hoping they would always be friends and her interests would never change.

Noah was hoping they would.

Chapter Six

"Is it possible to succeed without any act of betrayal?"

-Jean Renoir

By the time of his extended stay in a small town near Salt Lake City, Thomas had listened to three entire self-help programs from start to finish. He felt he had a firm grip on *Speaking Eloquently with Body Language*, he memorized every word of, *Mighty Memory* and he had gotten all he could from *How to Get Anything from Anyone* Now he was anxious to get moving on *New Body Now*.

However, he had more pressing problems than flabby abs. He had no car, nowhere to sleep and very little cash left from the robbery. He also had miles to go to get to his destination of Los Angeles.

There wasn't much in the trunk of the car that he wanted. All he had was clothes, and even they were disposable. He grabbed a pair of worn-out but comfortable boots, his two best shirts, a pair of jeans and a pair of dress pants, rolled them up and stuffed them into a backpack along with the CD collection.

Then he wiped his fingerprints from all of the surfaces and abandoned the valiant vehicle without further hesitation. His father had pried the VIN plate off the car after he stole it and had shown him how to make his own realistic-looking reusable temporary tag using a camera, a library printer and some clear contact paper. The car had not been legal in years and Wayne/Thomas had so far been lucky. He was glad to be rid of it.

He tucked his unruly hair up into his cap and walked quickly away from the heap. He was 50 yards from the car when saw an SUV approaching and stuck out his thumb.

"Where ya headin'?" an androgynous voice asked. The person matched the voice: Thomas wasn't sure if the question had come from a woman or a man. The person behind the wheel was wearing a loose, faded-denim shirt with pockets on the chest. He poked his head into the Subaru and noticed a big turquoise ring on a beefy hand with painted fingernails.
Painted nails: female. He decided to fake a stutter hoping that a speech impediment might make her uncomfortable enough not to ask too many questions. (Disk 4 of *How to Get Anything from Anyone*: "A handicap or sympathetic problem is the fastest way to a middle-aged woman's heart.")

"I was su-su-su-supposed to meet s-some friends at the ma-ma-mall, but my riiiiiide left without mmme." He lied hoping there was a mall within easy driving distance to give credence to his lie.

Again, and as usual, he was lucky.

"I'm going by there, put your bag in the back seat and hop in."

"Thank you m-m-ma'am."

"That your car back there?"

"N-no, I'm hhhhhhhoofin' it."

Did you see anybody in it?"

"N-n-no ma'am, it's eeeeempty."

"Wasn't there when I went by here an hour ago. Huh!" The woman looked ahead at the road, contemplating the stranger.

"S-s-s-somebody ssstopped to get him, but they d-didn't have room for mu,mu,me."

"Hitchhiking's not a very smart thing to do, even at your age," She said looking him up and down trying to decide of he was in his twenties or thirties.

"People die of dehydration out here and you don't look so good. I'm taking you to the side of the mall that has the food court. Go to the Super Smoothie. My brother owns it. You tell him Diane said to give you a smoothie. I'll call him, he'll be ready for you."

She circled her quiet air-conditioned SUV around to the far side of the mall and stopped in front of the entrance doors.

"I hope you find your friend." She said, smiling.

"It ssseems I fffound one m-ma'am. He grinned back. She might be a handy person to know if he had to stay for long. Best to be friendly.

The Mend

He picked up the smoothie that was waiting for him as promised. Diane's brother was not in the store, but he had called the assistant manager, a teenaged girl who handed him the cold, sweet drink and looked him up over. He knew he looked disheveled and dirty; he had not had a shower in a week but he had used deodorant and he hoped it was working. She didn't seem to notice and she smiled a shy smile.

He could tell she didn't meet many strangers. He nodded his thanks with a smile and backed away leaving her intrigued and took the drink to a table in the invisible middle of the food court.

There, he scanned the cavernous room until he found the perfect short-term employment situation. He went to the men's room, changed his shirt and ran a comb thought his hair before walking confidently to the counter of the largest food vendor in the court.

Peeking Chicken/ Burpin' Duck, a funny name for two restaurants side-by-side, was obviously run by one manager. A help-wanted sign was taped to both of the registers, which shared space on the spotless counter. Thomas looked for the manager hoping for a motherly type. The pity ploy seemed to work well in the Midwest and he was eager to try it again.

The only lesson in *How to Get Anything from Anyone* that had come close to preparing him for the manager he would face was "Only laugh at someone when they tell a funny joke."

At five feet tall, and weighing no more than ninety pounds, the thin, bespectacled Vietnamese manager was more authoritarian than he looked. His bleached white hair made him look insane and his curt, loud, one-word commands made his young American staff jump and obey.

"Go! He commanded and a young woman dashed to the register to which he was pointing.

"Dishes!" he snapped at another and she disappeared to the back.

Thomas held up the sign and asked if it was a good time for an interview. The man looked him up and down, nodded and gestured for Thomas to follow him to the cramped stock room that doubled as a break room.

On one side of the area was a sturdy set of steel shelves heavily stacked with boxes and extra cooking equipment that reached to the ceiling. A rickety, worn step-stool leaned against it. On the other side of the room was a small table, on which was a stack of napkins, a magazine with no cover, and a battered little radio/CD player. The radio in it was *almost* tuned to a country music station. The static made the room seem more private. The table also held a rack of blank employment applications and a coffee cup covered in multicolored stars that said, "Dream Big."
It seemed ironic or perhaps too hopeful in a mall food court in the middle of nothing important.

The Mend

There were only two chairs. The man took one and Thomas stood by the other one waiting to be asked to sit. (Disk 7 *Speak Eloquently with Body Language*: "In formal situations, show respect by only sitting when invited to sit.")

Once invited and seated, he still towered above his prospective boss. He wasn't sure the neuro-linguistic technique of mirroring he intended to use would work on someone so obviously different than himself.

He tried to make himself appear smaller. He tried narrowing his eyes, but then realized that if he used the simple rule, "Casually mimic the mannerisms of your quarry." He would come off looking like he was making fun of the man. If he didn't need the job, he was sure he would have.

He switched techniques and went with an advanced tip. He relaxed his body and maintained short periods of eye contact, being careful to look down and lean back a little when he felt the man move forward, an act of submission. He also put his hands on the table at the same distance and angle of the manager whose piercing wire-framed eyes never left Thomas' face. Thomas moved in a similar but not identical way. He was direct, confident and precise in his words. Slowly he started moving his hands first, almost imperceptibly in an attempt to shift the power position from the manager to himself. After all, he was the one looking for an employee.

The Mend

The manager's hands did indeed follow.

"Why should I hire you?" the man said.

"I think you should hire me because women like me and they buy most of the food at the mall for themselves and their kids." He grinned at the man and hoped there was an iota of gay in him. Physical attraction seldom failed him.

Thomas was grateful that genetics had given him his mother's face. She had given him nothing else. He only knew from a photo he found in a tattered Bible when he was looking for lost change under his father's dresser. Women liked his face; it had gotten him many first dates.

"I'm friendly and intelligent, I can work long hours, I don't mind being paid minimum wage, in cash if you like, and... I know how to spot a thief."
He stopped for a second to allow the last sentence to register with his prospective boss. The man looked as if he was wondering what he meant.
"For instance, the redheaded kid working the register is not ringing up single drinks when a customer pays with cash. Your problem is, they are one dollar including tax, no change required. They give him the dollar, he doesn't have to open the register he puts it on top of the drawer aaaand it's going straight in his pocket."
He said the last sentence just as the boy slipped a one-dollar bill into the wide pocket of his loose jeans.

The Mend

When he was Wayne, Thomas had done a variation of that same trick at an ice cream store called Dairy Dome before he was caught and fired.

From that episode, he learned to never pocket money during his shift but to take it out at the end when he counted his drawer.

He also learned to ring up a 50-cent fruit pie instead of a two-dollar shake and make half again the profit.

He ate a lot of free pies and watered down the shake mix to keep the inventory from giving him away.

He learned to spot a thief by being one.

The small manager looked at him sideways, walked over to the hapless redheaded boy, and jabbed his hand into his pocket. Several wadded-up dollar bills spilled out as the kid's face turned the approximate shade of his hair.

"Out!" He yelled and the kid, who had been speaking to a group of girls, (all of whom were now looking away in embarrassment) took off his apron and disappeared out the back door.

"Start now. Wash up. Gloves. Cut vegetables."

The man grunted as he went into his little office to fetch paperwork. Thomas decided use the name "Alan Miller" on his application. He knew he wouldn't be there long enough to be discovered and it was the most forgettable name he could come up with.

Thomas was beginning to feel grateful to Courtney. Since he had been using the tips on the CDs, he had gotten almost everything he wanted. Her self-help addiction was serving him well.

The next two months taught Thomas more than the CDs ever could. In the beginning, he used techniques from *Mighty Memory* to learn the names of everyone that visited Burpin' Duck regularly. People felt like he knew them and his tip jar was always full.

Some of the dollar bills were passed coyly across the counter with girls' names and phone numbers written on them. He ignored them.

Making friends and being remembered did not fit his long-term plan. He just wanted to make enough money to get to Los Angeles and start the real life he was planning in a notebook he kept in his backpack on the top shelf of the stockroom behind Christmas decorations.

He learned from *Speak Eloquently* to talk a little louder to older people while smiling and softer to a child bending to their eye level.

He learned to give women a little more space but then gradually move in until they gave him an indication that he was too close, then to back up slightly tilting his head to one side to show vulnerability.

He learned to start any conversation with a man his age or older in a confident but submissive posture, occasionally looking down and to the right.

The Mend

He learned not to make eye contact, but to show the inside of his wrists to gay men for instant connection without making it seem like he was coming on to them.

He used the ideas behind *How to Get Anything from Anyone* to talk the night security officer, who was just out of his teens, into allowing him to sleep free of charge, in the break/stock room on the nights he was working, and in the mall manager's supply room on nights when he wasn't, as long as he didn't get caught. Nights in the cold, stale rooms were spent working out vigorously to *New Body Now* followed by a few hours of strategic sleep.

Thomas adapted what he'd learned to his way of thinking and had developed new persuasion techniques that he hoped would make him a dangerous and powerful man. He polished his skills on people he knew were just passing through. When he felt confident in his abilities, he took bolder liberties.

How to Get Anything from Anyone helped him talk a young co-worker into adding a cell phone to his service when Thomas promised to pay the charges in advance for a year. Thomas got an untraceable phone, and the co-worker used the money to buy weed and a little coke, which he shared with Thomas.

The *Mighty Memory* tricks helped him memorize his boss's personal information from his employment application and used it to set up an online merchant account in his name. He used that account to charge all of the cards a "bank fee". No one questioned it and the small amounts added up quickly. He sometimes charged tourists with kids for things they didn't buy, they didn't have time to check their receipts, and if they did, he blamed it on a sticky cash register key.

New Body Now gave him the strength and coordination to quickly and painlessly break the Vietnamese manager's neck the day he discovered and confronted "Alan Miller" about the fake social security number, the merchant account and the fraudulent fees and charges.

Thomas took the man's glasses and put them in his pocket. They would make a good disguise later. (*How to Get Anything from Anyone*: "Glasses instantly change your face and give the appearance of intelligence. Add glasses for instant trust.")

After deleting all traces of his employment from the company computer, he removed his paper application from the desk file, effectively deleting all physical evidence he had ever been there.

He laid the stepstool on its side and only then did Thomas called for help. He shouted desperately, believably, wailing that he had just seen his boss fall off of the stepstool while trying to get a box from the top shelf.

"Overwhelmed by shock" over the sudden death of his mentor, he went to the bathroom where he put on a jacket and ball-cap from the lost and found that he had stashed in a ventilation grate for just this sort of emergency.

"Alan Miller" ceased to exist as Thomas Oni nee Wayne Walters walked out of the mall with only a notebook and a wad of cash.

The bank account he opened with his boss's information was bloated, he would be unable to take all of it now that his boss was dead, but he went to an ATM in a grocery store near the mall wearing a hid disguise, and withdrew the maximum, as he had every day for weeks and as he would do until the bank caught on to his boss's death and closed his account. He was confident he had enough money to live comfortably until he decided what to do next.

First, he would buy a cheap used car and drive to California, then he would set up a tax-free, barely accountable, *respectable* career and he would dominate.

The plan was to start his own church.

Chapter Seven

"Bullies want to abuse you. Instead of allowing that,
you can use them as your personal motivators.
Power up and let the bully eat your dust."

-Nick Vujicic

"I said back the fuck UP, what is wrong with you
retard? You sniffin' my meat?" The big guy had
puffed his chest up and was towering over Zack
Rubin, whose expression had not changed since he
was pushed back several feet from the line at the hot
dog vendor. "You want my wiener, queer kid?"

Zack stood his ground, neither pushing back nor
walking away. The bully shoved his shoulder into
Zack's, knocking him back a few more feet.

"Why are you doing this? You're twice my size."
Zack asked calmly. "I'm no threat to you."
"You're in my damned space. That's why. Get back.
In fact, you just get the hell out of here." The man
threw threatening glances at a few people who were
starting to stare in disapproval.

"I'm buying two hot dogs." Zack stood unafraid.
The second one was for Jen, who had gone to the

bathroom. She had been gone a long time. All of the important lines at the amusement park were long. He assumed the line to enter the bathroom was as well.

"You're getting out of here." The man insisted.

"I'm buying two hot dogs." Zack replied calmly.

"Not here." The bully pushed Zack to the ground.

Without a moment of hesitation, Zack quickly and efficiently put two fingers to one side and his thumb into the other of the bully's kneecap and twisted it firmly as he stood up. The big man fell to the ground screaming in agony.

Zack got up and calmly rejoined the scattering line of people at the hot dog vendor. The panicked vendor handed him two dogs, took no money in return, unplugged his cart and quickly rolled it away while two security officers and several onlookers surrounded the man and the boy.

A small crowd of people soon congregated.

Zack opened a pack of ketchup, spread it on his sandwich and wrapped Jen's in a napkin while the man continued holding his knee, screaming and pointing to Zack. He sat down on a bench and quietly ate his hot dog while one of the security guards assessed the situation and watched downloaded camera footage on her tablet.

From the angle of the camera, it looked exactly like the big guy pushed the little guy down and the little guy merely reached out for help regaining his feet in exactly the wrong location.

The bully's knee *had* helped Zack get to his feet; the twist, that he had learned watching forensic videos, was a last-second idea.

There are a lot of nerves running through the knee. Separating the patella from the knee joint pinches those nerves between the two and disables an opponent instantly. Zack thought correctly that disabling the threatening man was the logical choice to avoid further conflict.

When EMTs removed the big guy on a stretcher, those who had been there from the start of the bullying episode applauded.

Jennifer returned and Zack silently handed her the remaining hot dog.

"What in the heck just happened here?"

"That guy's going to need surgery."

"Did you do that?"

"I didn't intend to."

"How...what...explain!"

When she repeated the story to his father that evening, Eric knew it was time to institute some new lessons in Zack's life.

"This face..." Eric's computer screen showed a teen-aged girl looking forlornly into the camera.

"Is angry?" Zack asked.

"No. Sad." He clicked the forward button showing an older man scowling viciously.

"Sad?"

"No. Angry." Eric wanted to laugh but his son's inability to recognize the subtleties of emotion was a genuine worry.

"What do you do when you see this?" The computer showed a woman crying.

"Step back, hands visible, ask her if I can help?"

"Yes!" He was glad that the boy was naturally compassionate. This was the first time since he was a baby that he had shown any level of aggression.

"And when you see this?" The screen showed the rest of the picture, the woman was bleeding from a deep gash in her leg.

"Call 911, then tell her I need to apply pressure to the wound. Ask for permission."

"Yes! O.k. now... when you see this?" It was the scowling man again.

"Ask if I can help, step back, hands visible, apply pressure... just kidding! Step back, but stay aware, don't turn my back, and avoid prolonged eye contact."

"Yes! Very good! And… don't tear off his kneecap!" Eric shook his head.

They had been working on emotion recognition and response for nearly an hour when Eric suddenly fell unconscious to the floor.

Zack called 911 on Eric's phone, and simultaneously called Jennifer on his own just as Eric opened his eyes again and sat up.

"Can I help, Dad? What should I do?" Zack asked. He hoped his face didn't show how worried he was. His heart was thumping; the sound of it was whooshing rhythmically in his sensitive ears.

"I'm ok Zack, hang up your phone."

Jennifer answered as he said it, Zack thought quickly.

"I …just wanted to say goodnight." Zack stumbled. It was the first real lie he had ever told her, although the second she answered, he *did* want to say goodnight to her. It still felt wrong.

Eric took his phone back from the boy and placed it on a nearby coffee table then reached out to Zack for help off the floor.

"What just happened dad? You're not ok."

"I'm fine, I will explain later, but now I need rest."

Eric realized the 911 dispatcher was still on the phone. He canceled the ambulance and caught his breath. He had ben told his new medication had peculiar side effects and now he knew what at least one of them was. He would be more careful. He never wanted to see that look on his son's face again.

He thought about telling the boy what was happening, but he didn't want to worry him after the stressful day.

Zack went to his room to read. It was not one of his nights to sleep, and he wasn't tired, especially not now.

Chapter Eight

"If you really want to experience God,
go and make disciples."
- Francis Chan

Thomas had spent four months acting as a roadie for a musical gospel ministry. He had studied what worked and what didn't from both sides of the stage. He had a plan and he was ready to test it.

He sat alone at the bar while a rotund bar mistress played video games on her phone. He was ready put his Los Angeles plan in motion.

He had drunk only one beer, but he had been watching and eavesdropping on the three men at the pool table for an hour as he had every day for nearly a week and tonight they were finally drunk enough.

"Stop yellin' every damn thing you say, I got a headache and you're messin' up my game." complained a thin, squinty man with a transparent mustache who was lining up his shot wrong. He shot and missed the pocket by inches.

"God damn it, I'm goin' back to cards. He pouted.

The Mend

"You can't blame your sucky-ass game on a headache!" A top-heavy balding man in a t-shirt two sizes too small, scooped two five dollar bills off the table. "My back ain't been right for months and I'm still kicking your whiney ass."

The third man was quiet, hanging his entire upper body over his beer like he was protecting it from the light. The fat man nudged him and gestured for him to move further into the booth so he could sit down. He didn't budge.

Thomas moved closer and waited for them to notice him staring at them, but as they had every other night, they seemed oblivious.

His hair had not been cut in months, it hung well past his shoulders. It was newly-bleached white as were the clothes he was wearing. He knew that if he interrupted the men, he was a fist target.

He intended to be, but he was getting frustrated. It was taking longer than he thought it would. His plan relied on the sun shining.

He walked over to the outdated jukebox with two broken panels on the front and played Madonna's "Like a Prayer".

If that didn't do it, nothing would.

All three men looked up as the song began.

"What the fuck is that pansy-ass bullshit?" the fat man bellowed.

"Turn that shit off!" the thin man added.

The third man calmly got up, unplugged the jukebox and went to sit back down, but the fat man casually blocked his way and pointed to Thomas.

"That guy looks like your cousin David." The thin man said to the quiet one. "The one that likes it up the ass."

Finally. The insult was what Thomas was looking for. He continued to stare at the men as he plugged the jukebox back in.

"What are you looking at?" The thin man was walking toward him. Thomas didn't move. The other two moved toward him as well. Thomas looked directly into their eyes one at a time; it was a challenge and they knew it.

The thin man lurched toward him and pushed Thomas's chest knocking over his beer and making first contact.

That woke the bar maid from her game-induced stupor, she looked perturbed that she now had a mess to clean up and she didn't want more.

"Get out of here with that caveman attitude." she scolded as she scooped the beer off the counter with a bar rag and threw the bottle in the trash. She didn't want it used as a weapon.
"I mean it, get out!"

The Mend

Thomas backed out the door his palms to his face and his fingers motioning to the men to bring it on.

Once outside he let the fat man have the first blow. He allowed it to connected lightly with his shoulder and glance off, now he knew all of the man's strength was in his weight.

The fat man was cumbersome and slow, less coordinated than he thought he was. Nonetheless, emboldened by the first punch, he stepped back to recoil for another swing.
Thomas took a quick step in the direction of the raised arm. As the fist came toward him, he grabbed it and added to its momentum by pulling it to his side directing it safely out of range and knocking the big guy to the ground.

New Body Now had given him strength, but *Self Defense Shortcuts,* a DVD he bought after reaching California, taught him enough to make this work. He realized that had the men been sober, he would be vulnerable but that's why he waited and watched.

The thin man stepped in, kicking. Thomas let the first blow hit his hip, but as the man was pulling his leg back to regain his balance, he kicked the other one out from under him sending him sprawling onto his friend who had almost gotten up before he was toppled over again.

The third man stood by smiling and watching. He seemed to be in no hurry to defend his compadres.

"Nothing? You just gonna stand there?" Thomas needed this guy to fight the most, he had seen the veteran license plate on his Jeep so he knew he was ex-military and he wondered what he could do.

He didn't have to wait long, the man erupted into fists and feet. Thomas was not prepared for that kind of speed and fury and he was pummeled badly before he finally hit the dirt. The third man laughed.

Seeing an opportunity, Thomas kicked the drunk man's legs behind his knees and brought him down opposite the other two who were watching from the ground. He stood quickly, his back to the sun, his foot on the third man's throat.

His plan had worked. The most capable among them was prone, his neck pressed against the corner of the curb rendering him helpless. He was no longer the leader, Thomas was.

"Gentlemen." Thomas said, "I've come to help you. Let's talk."

The two facing him were stunned into silence, their eyes wide in disbelief. He had calculated his position for the perfect effect. Where he stood the sun was at his back, causing its light to refract off of his shirt and his chemically-lightened hair. With his slightly bent arms raised to his sides in a wide-open gesture, the sun shone through his sheer sleeves.

He shimmered like an angel. The violet blue of his eyes stared as if into their darkest thoughts. The bridge of the song was filtering out of the saloon like an anthem. "I hear you call me name and it feels like home."

"Or I could end this."

The fat guy nodded his surrender and Thomas stepped off his friend's throat. Now he knew the pecking order: the vet, the paunchy man, and then the thin man.

All three got to their feet and looked around to see that no one had witnessed their humiliation. They composed themselves, checked for damage and followed him back inside.

Thomas tossed a ten on the bar for the pot of coffee, took it from the machine and walked to the table where the drunk men were sitting down. He didn't pull up a chair.

"Try these on." He said to the squinty, thin man and he pulled the glasses he had stolen from his murdered boss, months earlier from his backpack on a barstool. "They might cure your headaches."

The man looked at him with doubt but took them anyway and put them on. A half smile crossed his face. He had not realized how bad his eyes had gradually gotten but suddenly everything was clear and sharp.

"Give me your wallet." he said to the fat man.

"Fuck you, man. We'll go back outside, just me and you" He had thought about what he had done wrong in the fight and remembered he had a handgun in his car. He was ready for round two.

Thomas leaned down and looked him in the eye, his hand slowly curling.
The other two men leaned back, signaling they would not join a new fight. The fat man backed down as well and placed his hand in his pocket over his wallet.

"Where am I gonna go with it? Give me your wallet." Thomas said it softly.

The man relinquished his wallet. Thomas took it with one hand and passed his other hand over it as if blessing it, then handed it back. "Put it in your front pocket, sitting on it is effecting your spine."
A realization seemed to occur to the fat man; it was the answer to where his back pain was coming from.

"You." he said to the third man, "Give me your phone." It was handed over without delay. The third man knew he was too wasted to win.

Thomas looked down the short list of contacts and found what he was looking for listed: "Ashlee" with two e's. definitely young. He clicked the call button and got a high-pitched voicemail message as he knew he would. During late afternoon on a weekday, Ashlee would still be in school. Her voice told him she was not a wife or girlfriend, but a daughter. He ended the call without leaving a message and texted the number instead.

> "Ash, I've been sick for a while, but I am on the mend. Don't give up on me, even if you don't hear from me for a while. Everything will be better soon."

All three men gave their full attention to Thomas for the rest of the evening as he told them about their future and what great things they would soon accomplish together, and then they set about making it happen.

Chapter Nine

"All I want is good, honest, loyal friends."
-Aviv Nevo

Ideas for their last summer before college were escaping the three teenagers. Classes had already been over for three days. They looked at the next 12 weeks as one last chance to just be kids. They had one last summer before they had to decide who they were going to be, possibly for the rest of their lives.

"How about we backpack across Europe?" Jennifer said, and all three erupted into laughter. They were all kids of single parents, two of them were too poor to even consider Europe without having a job there.

Noah technically had two parents alive but his mother had left when he was a small child and his father had been too ill to work for over a year.

Jennifer's mother made good money as a nurse, but she had put most of into a college fund for her daughter.

Zack's father had done the same with a fund for graduate school. As a retired professor, Zack was guaranteed a scholarship. He had earned two bachelor's degrees and timed his entry into graduate school to coincide with the departure of his two best friend. Eric had also spent a small fortune on lessons, equipment, travel and other distractions for Zack, leaving him enough to live on, but to Zack's knowledge, not a lot more.

"What about music festivals?"

Noah knew before the words had even crossed his lips that Zack could never deal with the noise and uncontrolled chaos that a music festival entails.

He wore earplugs to Jennifer's piano and dance recitals and sat in the back row even when the venue was nearly empty.

"I actually have enough money that we all COULD backpack if you wanted to…"
Jennifer and Noah burst into laughter. Zack had never held a job, they were sure he was kidding, which was not like him. Zack looked confused and moved on.
"I saw these on a forum and they look interesting."
Zack posted a list of summer experiences that were low-cost or free on the screen above them.

First was an internship opportunity working on a field crew in a national forest. The original forum poster had jokingly nicknamed it "The Poison Ivy Initiative".
"Too isolated." Jennifer said." No wi-fi!"
"But so peaceful!" Zack added. He liked the quiet of nature.

Jennifer and Noah shook their heads.

The next one on the list was an opportunity to earn college credits tutoring inner-city kids. The post had named it "Prison Prevention Project" Zack didn't need the credits and he noticed the other two didn't look interested.

"Club MEND?!" Noah read ahead. "That sounds like a copyright case in the making!" He read the opening paragraph and scanned the list of activities the summer program was offering.

No archery or canoeing at this program; everything they offered was cerebral but looked like fun. Virtual reality programming rooms, art classes, advanced music classes, and video production stoked the imaginations of the three. "But there is no *price* here."

"It's free, but you have to test into it, unless you have a disability. The catch is, you have to spend some time volunteering with the disabled people in the program."

"That's cool. Think I could fake paralysis? Then you two could take care of me!" Noah didn't take more than a second to think about it; 'free' was all he needed to hear.

"Brain damaged maybe!" Jennifer was still reading. She could see no downside. "Where do you take the test?"

"It's online, they give you the results immediately. Looks like there are still some spots available. If you think it would be fun, we should give it a go. If we are all in that is, I'm not going unless you are going."

"Hecks yes!" Noah pulled his tablet out of his backpack and Jennifer clicked open her phone. Zack typed into the wireless keyboard to the overhead screen and with that, they all signed in.

"Ready, set, go!" Jennifer said. They all knew Zack would be the first one to complete the application followed by Jennifer, then Noah.

They filled in the usual form questions concerning name, address and phone number, then answered oddly detailed questions about their health, lifestyle and activity level.

It seemed strange that the questionnaire asked for the occupations of siblings, grandparents, aunts and uncles. None of the three had any.

Noah lied and said his mother was dead. He would soon be 18 and he thought of himself as an adult, he didn't want an unsigned permission slip or his mother's unavailable income information to wreck the opportunity.

Finally, they were asked to watch a video with their cameras focused on their faces and answer questions about what they had seen afterward.

On every screen was a different video, each a bizarre montage of sounds and images. In some animals and people merged together a twisted hybrid of intertwined images and sound that none of them could understand.

There were flashes of color, some labeled with the wrong color name, and three-dimensional geometric shapes that formed optical illusions. There were flowers aflame, and some that appeared to be growing underwater and in the air. Although the video was only one minute in duration, when asked its length in the questionnaire, Noah would recount that it was half an hour long, Jennifer would answer fifteen minutes.

The questionnaire phase of the video baffled Zack's friends but he clicked through the 30 questions in half a minute and went to get a glass of chocolate milk.

When he returned the other two were still considering the questions, so he went back to the kitchen to bring back a plate of shortbread and two more glasses of milk for them.

"O.k. ready to hit the result button?" He asked as he sat down.

"I already did, I got in!" Noah seemed stunned; the test seemed far too difficult for him to have passed.

"I'm ready." Jennifer said, confident that if Noah got in they would all be going together. There were still 4 spaces when they had begun the test. Her phone pinged. "In!" She grinned.

Zack cleared his throat and clicked.

"Congratulations and condolences. Our test shows you are better suited for our Leadership Academy. Unfortunately, all spots for the Leadership Academy have been filled. Please try earlier next year." Zack sat motionless as he read his screen. By succeeding, he had failed the test.

"No damned way!" Noah was shocked but not disappointed; secretly he was overjoyed. He wanted the opportunity to spend some time with Jennifer away from Zack. He hoped it would make her finally notice how much he liked her, maybe she would like him back.

"We could still backpack across Europe." She offered again meekly, this time no one laughed. "We will figure something out."

"We could you know, like I was saying about money…" Zack stammered, he didn't know if his friends would laugh again.

"C'mon! Free program! Virtual reality rooms! Noah coaxed. "Brainiac could visit us, it's just 4 weeks, and we have 8 more at the end of summer." Noah saw his opportunity slipping away.

"You should go." Zack said without emotion. "It might be a great opportunity. You've never been out of Ohio. I've got a lot of things to do here. Pop hasn't been feeling well lately and I was sort of thinking of doing a research project for him. I'll be fine, there is no sense in your wasting this summer on my account."

Noah's heart leapt, the program was in California, that meant he had the plane ride there and back alone with Jennifer, and they could schedule some of the same activities too. With no Zack to compare him to, she could see that he could be more than just a friend.

"It's a moot point until we run this by our parents anyway." He said resignedly. He knew his dad would be glad he was going and Jennifer's mom, Debbie, was dating a new man, she would probably welcome the privacy.

"You sure this is o.k. with you?" Jennifer asked. In those few times in which she couldn't tell what he was thinking, if she asked, he would always tell the truth.

"Seriously, I'm good. I haven't had time to get my heart set on it. The Mend sponsors it, they're getting good press. I hear they are doing amazing things. This could be good for you. Go."

Jennifer and Noah both accepted their places for fear they would be snapped up by someone else.

Jennifer's phone pinged again. Her e-ticket had been purchased; the plane would leave in 17 hours. If she wanted to go she had less than a day to get ready.

Noah's tablet pinged. His flight was leaving first thing in the morning. He sighed audibly. Since they wouldn't be traveling together, he would just have to make up for lost time once they got to the workshop.

"Wow, that's fast. They don't procrastinate, do they?" He put his tablet back in his bag and swung it over his shoulder as he stood up, grabbed two pieces of shortbread and moved toward the door.

"You're my ride." He motioned to Jennifer. "I've got to tell my dad and pack."

"I'll be there in a second." Jennifer said without looking in his direction. "Are you 100% sure this is ok with you?" She asked Zack.

"If you're asking me if I'm disappointed, yes, I am. But I can tell you I will be just fine, and I really do hope you have a wonderful time."

Even as he said the words, his mind became uneasy. It was happening too fast. They had been given no time to research. He wrote it off as disappointment and smiled at Jennifer as she opened the door to leave. "See you tomorr.... see you later!"

He called after her. It was going to be a long four weeks without her.

After his friends left, Zack shared his shortbread and the news with his father, then went to his bedroom. He didn't sleep.

For the next seven days, Zack threw himself into projects to try not to miss them, but something was nagging at him. Apparently, the same thing was starting to bother his father.

"Zack, what did you say was the actual name of that workshop?" Eric's brow was furrowed when Zack walked in the office.

"I don't know its actual name, it was nicknamed 'Club Mend' on the forum. It's run by The Mend, that Techno-evangelical movement in California."

Eric didn't like the speed at which his son's friends had gone either and had started to research the facility. So far, he had found nothing untoward. No lawsuits, no accusations, and no scandals but the URL for the questionnaire he had found in the computer's history now returned a DNS error. Even the forum posting was gone. The second it was full, the program didn't officially exist anywhere anymore. It seemed odd to both of them.

"What do you know about this 'Mend'?"

"I've been reading about it. It is a non-profit, but not quite a church, not yet. It's 16 or 17 years in operation."

"Why have I not heard about it?"

"It's sciency. Not your thing. Thomas Oni, the man that founded it is a major donor to DNA research labs. Apparently, they are pioneering new ways to treat crippling disabilities. I guess it is sort of like a medical science church."

"That's such a contradiction, it makes my head spin." Eric shook his head.

"They hold Saturday meetings all over the world. They also do seminars for corporate types." Zack pulled up the web page and they looked at pictures of people The Mend had helped while looking for a photo of Thomas Oni the founder and director.

There were before and after photos of people in wheelchairs and hospital beds standing confidently after going through a four-week healing process ending in a sort of baptism called "The Wash". The "after" photos were stunning in their differences to the before photos.

"Looks like a cult to me." Eric thought but didn't say the words out loud. He didn't want to upset his son with his only friends involved, but he was starting to worry. The kids had been gone a week, and outside of one scripted text explaining that they had agreed to give up their phones in order to spend full time exploring the program, no one had heard from them.

Finally, a close up of Oni appeared on the screen and Eric froze. He knew the face in the photo and he knew it well. There was no mistaking those unique eyes. For once he was glad his son had a hard time reading faces. This one looked too much like his own.

He sent Zack to order pizza and set about reading all he could about Thomas Oni and The Mend. When he had read every word on the web page, he looked though his Rolodex for the number of his old friend Martin Anderson and invited him over for drinks.

Martin had been on his way home after picking up take-out to get him through his wife's yoga night. He left the food in the car and met his old friend at the front door.

Martin had been the officer assigned to investigate the accident that had taken Eric's wife. His own daughter had been the same age as Catherine and something about seeing Eric zipping his baby girl inside his coat against his warm shirt, tucking her head under his chin to protect her from the freezing rain had bonded the two. He had ushered Eric away from the mangled car that from one side looked untouched and had put the two in his squad car. He had promised to update them as soon as EMTs had freed his wife. She was trapped inside the gracefully unseen other side of the car.

The update he delivered was the most crushing of his career. She was dead. They would later find she had been pregnant. Eric always wished they had not told him it was a boy.

Years later, Zack had taken some of the sting out of those memories, but now, as Eric hugged his old friend hello, those memories were coming back.

He remembered how helpless he had been to turn the car when the headlights were bearing down on them though the rain.
Although he had seen the old brown car careening toward them and had grabbed the wheel as hard as he could, he had only managed to keep one half of the car safe as the other half lurched up onto the guard rail, and post after post wracked his wife's body, flinging it around inside her seatbelt like a crazed exploding marionette.

The split-second decision had saved only two lives and had allowed him a few more years with Catherine, but now she too was a bittersweet memory.

Martin stepped back from the hug and looked a bit alarmed when he saw Eric. The older man was not how he had known him. The loose lavender skin and visible cheekbones under sagging eyes merely whispered of the past vitality of the robust, athletic man Martin was expecting. Thinking of the losses he had endured, Martin understood, but there was something more...

"Dad, I need another ten." Zack's head popped around the corner. "Oh, hello."

"Martin, this is my son Zack. Zack, Martin Anderson and I are old friends. Could you set another plate at the table please?"

"Dad, it's pizza. Who eats pizza at the table?"

"I had a couple of egg rolls in the car," Martin said as he glanced at the delivery car that had just pulled up, "but if that's Vincenza's, I'll force myself."

"It IS Vincenza's! One is a mushroom-sausage Sicilian." Zack exclaimed, "Coke or Sprite? Beer?"

"Beer, and make that two, Zack. I could use one tonight." Eric handed him the second ten-dollar bill and Zack disappeared to return thirty seconds later to drop a pizza box, two beers and three paper plates in front of the men.

Eric returned to the conversation.

"It's good to see you Martin, I'm sorry I haven't kept in touch more than through Christmas cards but I've been really busy," He nodded toward Zack. "I'm sure you have too. How are Alyssa and Joan?"

"And Marty!" Martin grinned. He opened his wallet showing a photo of a grinning curly-haired boy with a dirty face. "He was a sneak attack, five years old, outta the blue!" Joan is fine. Alyssa is living in Euclid with her husband and they are about to give us another little sneak attack in June."

"A grandchild, wow." Eric was pleased to find Martin's life was going so well. The last time they had talked Martin and Joan were considering a divorce, things had obviously gotten better.

The three sat down and the two caught up. Zack inhaled his first piece of pizza, all the while penciling in the margins of a textbook on holographic technology. He took two more slices with him to his room, and the men got down to business.

"I want to know about someone and I don't know where to start. I don't think a background check is going to be enough but I'd like to start there."

"I can help you with that. Do you have a computer handy?" Eric squeezed the remote in his hand and the tv screen came to life. The photo of Thomas Oni was still on the television, which doubled a computer monitor. Eric handed a wireless keyboard to Martin, and he logged into his department's research software. "Is that the guy you are looking at?"

"His name is Thomas Oni. Apparently, he's a famous television evangelist type."

"I recognize his face. Isn't that the miracle guy who can cure diseases? I read about him. They don't know how he does it and he's got a patent on his process so he's not tellin'."

He typed the name into the search form and carefully looked up and down the page.

"Huh. This guy didn't get his social security card until he was 28 years old. He's either a late bloomer or he lived somewhere he didn't have to drive. I'm not seeing any state ids, no bank records, no school information; no hospital records... nothing until 17 years ago. He ain't 17. Something's not right about that. People can have new names, but that doesn't affect their social security numbers."

"Are you saying that Thomas Oni is not his real name?"

"If not, he was born when he was 28 years old. We've got laws, you have to have a social security card right after you're born or to get a driver's license or when you get a job."

"How could we find out who he was?

"Only way I know is if he's got DNA on file. That would mean he committed a crime. He would have to voluntarily or by court order give you his DNA and we could check it in the FBI database."

"No other way?"

"Well, if he was reported as a missing person, that might be a lead, but you would be looking at 17 years of some really old files, mostly on microfiche." Martin finished his second slice and washed it down with the last of his beer. "You got a lot of ink in that printer? 'cause I can't leave this logged in."

Eric suddenly thought about the policeman's family, how close he was to retirement and how if this somehow became more than they intended, he might lose his job. He had enough to go on for the moment so he decided to drop it. "Maybe we could just print out the missing men from Cleveland around that time."

"What makes you think he's from here?"

"I think I might know his family."

As a public-school teacher, Eric knew members of many families.

When he became a professor, he had a lot of his former students in his classes again and gotten to know them well.

Martin didn't question the explanation, until Zack returned to the room. His face was positioned side by side with the photo of Oni still up on the screen.

"Did you know that with perfect lighting most people can't tell today's holograms from reality?" He interrupted.

Both men were looking intently at him. He backed up a step. "Never mind?" He rolled his eyes and disappeared back to his room.

Martin immediately knew what the connection to Oni was without a doubt, but he kept his mouth shut and printed paperwork from 17 years earlier.

After he had gone, it didn't take long for Eric to find what he was looking for: an unlocated person of interest report filed in response to a complaint on behalf of Loretta Walters: deceased.

Eric recognized the name. The coincidence seemed unfathomable. Wayne Walters, the suspect, was Loretta's brother.

He called the police department's non-emergency line and asked for a young officer who had been one of his students. He told her that he needed the entire file for an academic paper and he reminded her that it was public record. It took her half an hour to find it, but she emailed the report to him.

Melissa Byers, the friend who filed the complaint suspected Loretta's brother, Wayne, in her death. She revealed that Loretta had told her an awful secret: she had been raped by her brother. Miss Byers feared Wayne had come back to kill his sister to protect their secret. Since Loretta's death had already been ruled a natural death due to childbirth, and since the rape had been unreported by the alleged victim, the over-worked officer on duty had decided not to investigate. Her death had been confirmed by autopsy. No other injuries. No way it was murder. He didn't want to do the paperwork. No one followed up.

A sickening thought crossed Eric's mind that had not occurred to the officer. Wayne Walters could be Thomas Oni and if so, Thomas Oni was Zack's uncle

and if he had indeed raped his sister *possibly also his father*. He clicked on classfriends.com and looked through area yearbooks for the years before Zack was born. There he was.
Wayne Walters looked very much like Thomas Oni. His hair was darker, but Eric's had been dark when he was young too. Wayne had been voted, "Most Likely to Host a Local Cable Show." by his class. His smarmy smile had not changed. The eyes were unmistakable but Loretta had the same eyes.

Zack's DNA had been called unusual.

Eric's breath left him for a moment and he had to sit down and think. He decided to keep his repulsive and unproven theory from his son. He was tired and he would figure out what to do about Zack's friends in the morning.

His mind was overloaded.

As he went to a disturbed and fitful sleep that night Eric forgot three things.

1. Zack seldom slept.

2. Computer forensics was his hobby, and

3. Zack always had a deep curiosity for anything Eric was doing.

Chapter Ten

"Physical courage, which despises all danger,
will make a man brave in one way;
and moral courage, which despises all opinion,
will make a man brave in another."
-Charles Caleb Colton

The shift in air pressure from someone opening and
closing the front door of the old brownstone rattled the
loose windows in his room and awakened Eric at 5:15
am. He put on his robe and shoved his feet into his
slippers to find out why.

As he walked past the living room on the way to
the door, the safety chain hanging from it was still
moving slightly but he didn't notice it. He glanced to
his left and saw that the protected screen Martin
Anderson had been so careful to sign out and close was
open again. He sat down and clicked through the tabs,
which included the local police department's portal to
the FBI database and several files therein concerning
Thomas Oni and The Mend.

What disturbed him most was hundreds of "before
and after" photos his son connected of people who had
been healed by The Mend.

He had arranged them in a logical way to form a

bigger picture drawing on his subconscious, as was his habit. The photos, when seen from a distance, formed a skull.

He rushed to the door knowing what he would, or rather wouldn't find when he opened it. Sure enough, his car was gone. Zack was just learning to drive; Eric felt he wouldn't risk driving alone without a license, but he rushed to Zack's room and found it empty.

He slipped into his clothes and grabbed his cell phone from his nightstand on his way back down the stairs, hitting redial and waiting to hear Martin's voice.

"Detective Anderson, I mean... hello."

"Martin we need to talk ...right away!" His voice crackled,

"It's 5:30 in the morning."

"Zack got into your files and he's gone."

Martin's voice went from irritated to concerned. Considering the content of last night's conversation, he knew better than to discuss it further on the phone. "I'll be right there."

He drove on nearly-empty streets noticing a few streetlights flickering off as the rest of the city woke up with less urgency. He was at Eric's door in fifteen minutes.

The television, with the still open screens was visible through the living room window and Martin's stomach knotted when he realized that his private login had been reused. It would look like he had been accessing the FBI database illegally off the clock. He could lose his job. The kid was a hacker!

"What the hell!" He tried not to show his annoyance but his job was on the line and he was ready to retire.

"I'm sorry Martin, Zack is incredibly intelligent. He must have a keystroke reader installed on this computer. He knows more than we do at this point and that's a lot and it's not good.

I did some research after you left. Please sit down." He motioned for Martin to sit in front of the screen and he picked up the keyboard to start from the beginning.

"Zack's mom was just a teenager when I found her in the park. She bled to death delivering him. Her parents were both dead and they couldn't find any other family members. Apparently, she had one. A half-brother, his name was Wayne Walters.

If the officer that took a statement from one of her friends had done his job, I wouldn't have Zack now, he would." He pointed to Oni on the screen.

"Probably best they didn't find him; according to that report, the girl's brother could also be Zack's father. He disappeared just before Oni appeared. Walters had a rap sheet for breaking and entering, check fraud, theft, forging prescriptions, and assault; all of it before he turned 18. That is closed to the local police now because he was a juvenile but Zack found it in federal files. He knows that Wayne Walters is Thomas Oni and that he is his uncle.

Martin looked sick. Eric forced himself to continue.

"Oni's movement, as you know is called The Mend and it has become powerful. Its members include people in important places. According to FBI files, which Zack has now read, Oni is marginally connected to missing people, arson, drug trafficking and more, but the investigations never get very far."

"He seems like the kind of guy who would be connected." Martin nodded as he spoke, trying to put the pieces together before he had them all.

"Yeah, and he knows how to get to local law. These files show serious connections in high places. I've seen photos of him with actors, musicians, foreign dignitaries and senators." Eric sighed.

"He's a hot shot. If he's done something wrong we've got our work cut out for us. It's not so easy to bust a hotshot. You've got to bring in outside forces and you have to have enough information to convince a DA. They won't make fools of themselves over this guy."

Eric continued. "That might be the case. I've got nothing but suspicions right now. The reason this is so urgent is that, as you can see Zack is extraordinarily intelligent. What you can't see is that he is also autistic. He tends to fixate on a problem and he will stop at nothing until the problem is repaired to his satisfaction. His problem right now is that his two best friends are in a program, run by The Mend and the entire program has disappeared. Now so has he."

"Disappeared?" Martin was confused.

"Yes, I can find no trace of it anywhere online or otherwise. His two best friends signed up through a link in a forum. That link has vanished, and now Zack and the two kids have vanished as well."

"Have their parents reported them missing?

"Not yet, they texted to say they were giving up their phones. They haven't been in contact with anyone since. They could be fine, I was hoping that was the case but after reading this, I don't think so."

"The first step to getting to the bottom of this is to report the kids missing, do you have contact information for their parents?"

"Yes, Noah's father lives just down the block, we should probably talk to him first. Jennifer's mother will be getting off work soon, we can drop by her place then."

"You got any coffee? It's six o'clock in the morning." Martin had just rolled out of bed.

Eric fetched the coffee in paper go-cups, including one for Noah's father who would probably be asleep. Martin looked over the remaining tabs on the screen. Eric could hear the keyboard and came back to see Martin looking at a flight to California that just left. Eric knew his son was on that flight. The Bitcoin account information on the one remaining tab showed a zero balance. Zack had moved the equivalent of $174,000 to liquid dollar funds. It was money Eric didn't even know he had.

It was too late to catch the flight. They set off down the street to see if they could get address information from Noah's father.

The lights were already on and the television was loud as they knocked on the front door. No one answered so they rang the doorbell and knocked louder. Still no response. Martin quickly walked around to the back door to knock.

A few moments later he opened the front door from inside. Behind him Noah's father lay on the floor. It looked and smelled as though he had been dead for a few days. An empty pill vial lay half under his body. The glass with which he had taken the overdose sat dry and upright on a side table.

Eric's mind raced. He had to get to Jennifer's mother and warn her, just in case this wasn't an accident.

That's when they both heard the sirens.

She had died instantly. Her car was found at the bottom of a hidden embankment. The police report would say she fell asleep at the wheel, two days earlier.

Chapter Eleven

"Every minute brings new opportunity. Every
minute brings new growth, new experiences."
-Mario Cuomo

The thumping music in the expansive auditorium was
energizing. Colorful banners hung overhead every 20
feet in the big hallway where small groups of people
were congregating at tables.

Jennifer's guide ushered her small group past
several smiling people wearing headsets and polo shirts
emblazoned with a version of the "Caduceus" staff and
snake symbol, commonly used by the American
Medical Association. ▌A man's bare body replaced the
winged rod.

The kids were excited to sign in, and anticipation
was building for the orientation ahead. They noticed
that everyone wearing a green shirt was leading a group
wearing green badges, and those wearing yellow shirts
were leading groups with yellow badges. Everyone had
a colorful badge and there were distinct differences
between the groups.

Jennifer could not define the differences but they
were there. Attitudes, behaviors, even hair styles
seemed to separate the colors. Those few guests with
purple badges were separated physically by a privacy
barrier from the rest. She caught a glimpse of them

being led to the auditorium's balconies through a private door.

She walked with a group of three other kids that had ridden with her on a private bus from the airport. Each attendee had been met by a guide who asked for the attendee's identification and cell phone, on which was their confirmation codes. Jennifer thought it was odd that their IDs and phones had not been returned.

Each guide entered a short text message in the phones, then turned them off and put them in labelled manila envelopes, promising to return them with an explanation later, "due to privacy concerns".

It started to make more sense as the bus passed through iron security gates embedded in stone walls nearly obscured by carefully manicured ivy. The campus was a well-protected expansive mansion.

To Jennifer it looked like a former factory made charming by technology inspired architectural touches. LED lights framed the windows, a video reader-board welcomed them with fireworks and classical music set to a dance beat emanated from weatherproof speakers.

The building sat on a rocky cliff overlooking the ocean but well away from the shore.
The group was hurried through the crowd that was multiplying in the lobby of the compound. Jennifer had not been able to talk to anyone except her cheerful blond guide who had not stopped talking since the airport. She had not seen Noah anywhere.

She wasn't sure she would, there were thousands of people passing quickly through several sets of double doors at the entrance.

Her guide led her to a table and she picked up a badge with her name on it. It was green and she noticed that most were yellow. The volunteers, who were busily directing people wore blue shirts and badges. Those who were working as security were wearing brown.

A few gold badges were handed to people exiting a limousine at another private door by a stern looking assigner who was checking his guest list carefully. He denied entrance to two of the women who were escorting the accepted guests, and brown-shirted boys showed them to what looked, through the briefly open door to be a well-supplied green room.

She scanned her table for Noah's name but there were so many books, that his name was not visible, but neither was hers.

Her blue-badged guide noticed her confusion over the colors, grabbed her by the hand and said, "I was once a Green! Come on, let's find our seats!" but offered no further explanation.

She ushered Jennifer down a long, sloped, carpeted aisle to near the front of hundreds of rows of seats. They were greeted by smiling people who nodded or waved at them all the way to their chairs.

The Mend

The music, which seemed unbearably loud, became less echoing as they took their seats. It softened to one pleasantly wavering chord that grew again in volume as the last of the audience shuffled to their seats and then it stopped. The doors at the rear of the auditorium were closed with a solid iron thud.

A drumbeat started and people began to clap along. The tempo increased as people clapped faster, and just as it started to blend into one mass of applause, it too stopped.

"Ladies and Gentlemen THOMAS ONI!" boomed a man's voice from the speakers.

The music began again, accompanied by strobe lights in all colors, as the crowd jumped to its feet clapping and chanting: "O-NI! O-NI! O-NI!"

A tall, slender but fit man whose thick, smooth, white hair laid on his shoulders, stood on a white platform that descended from the ceiling above a network of scaffolding and lights, his arms wide in an anticipatory embracing gesture. Opalescent lights played across his loose, white clothing. With 15 years practice, Thomas had mastered the illusion of appearing as a celestial being.

He grabbed the air over his head to the left as his platform neared stage level, and the left side of the audience let out a roar of applause and cheers. He made the same gesture to the right and they too cheered wildly.

Finally, when the platform landed in the middle of the stage, he stood with his arms open to the entire screaming, whistling audience. As he lowered his arms slowly the crowd became quieter but not silent. He leaned forward into his microphone.

"Why are you here?" he whispered, then paused. The crowd slowly grew still. Oni waited a few seconds for effect and repeated the question again, at barely a whisper. It was so quiet Jennifer could hear the boy beside her breathing.

"Are you here to be instructed about how to live your life?"
A few quiet murmurs could be heard. One man broke through loudly. "No!"

"Are you here to be shamed about who you are?" The objections were louder.

"Are you here because someone sent you as a punishment?" The man with the loud "no" yelled, "Hell no!"

"Who does that?" Several people laughed and all sorts of words were called out: Parents! Teachers! Bosses! Churches!

"This is not a school, I am not your boss, and THIS IS NOT A PREHISTORIC CHURCH!" Thomas stormed the words. "If you're here for the INDOCTRINATION, SHAMING, PUNISHMENT of an outdated religion, you're in the wrong place! GO HOME NOW!"

The applause was thunderous. Some whooped, some stomped, some whistled, no one left.

"But. If you're here to improve your future, stay and celebrate your place among us. Laugh, clap, MOVE!!" Techno-dance instrumental boomed through the speakers. Everyone in colorful polo shirts grabbed a dance partner from the audience and pulled them to the aisles. People in wheelchairs and behind walkers were pulled out into the aisles as well and were supported as they swayed or wheeled around in celebration.

The whole place undulated with people as cameras captured the best dancers and featured them on a giant screen above the stage. Some people looked around to play to the cameras that were moving back and forth on wires above them. Awareness of the cameras improved everyone's dancing and very few remained seated.

"I was just checking and now I see that we've got the best group ever here today! Now that everyone is on their feet, I want to see who you are. Don't move." Thomas gestured to the audience who screamed in approval. Thomas then addressed them quietly.

"If you're here to figure yourself out, you can sit down, we can help you with that." Several people sat down.

"If you're here to improve your money situation, you can sit down, we can help you with that." More than half the standing audience sat down.

"If you don't know why you are here, it's o.k. you can sit down, we will figure that out later." People laughed. All but fifty people were now seated.

"If you were invited by one of our online programs, you can sit down, we've got good things in store for you too." Thirteen people remained.

"Everyone still standing and those of you who can't stand in the aisles, if you are here for healing. Please make your way up to the stage." Three people looked confused that they had missed their cue to sit down and took their seats. The rest made their way to the stage.

As they reached the stage, the platform that Thomas was standing on rolled back smoothly without a sound revealing a large round pool with a spiral ramp leading to the deep middle. Steam coming off the water revealed that it was warm. The swimming pool scent of chlorine reached Jennifer's nose. She'd always loved the smell.

"As out of the life-giving, water-filled womb from which we came, we can be born again into this world. New. Healthy. Washed of all the damage the world has done to our bodies and minds. We can go into the wash and come out clean, unburdened by our past, free to begin life again, in the body we SHOULD have had, in the body we WOULD have had, if we had been able to find our own way to manifest that in our lives."

The crowd applauded at the pause.

"But we can't always do it alone. You are all here to help manifest that now for these people." Thomas nodded to one of the people standing in a line beside him. "We will go into the healing waters of The Wash together and you will come out CLEARED of the misery of your past. If you are ready to be CLEAR and go willingly, you will come out new. If you are not chosen, it will only be because you are not ready. When you are ready, I will know, and you will go."

Jennifer looked to her guide for an explanation but the girl was looking straight ahead at Thomas.

"If you are chosen and choose not to go into the healing Wash but to stay with this life, that's o.k. too but know this, there is a better way."

Thomas approached the group that now stood instinctively closer together.

"Please come to me and let me look into your eyes, let me see if the terrible pain you have endured, the long agony of your life has been enough to make you ready to give up your past completely. Let me see if you are ready to enter The Wash and come out new and clean." He walked down the short line of people tapping three of them on the shoulder and motioning the rest to the side of the stage.

"I don't want any of you to feel you are being left out. We will not abandon you." He looked to the audience that was hanging on his every word.

"Can I get to you come together as one and send these people courage to do what they need to do, to heal their lives? Let me hear it."

Polite applause filtered up to the stage.

"I'm going to need you to mean it." Thomas chastised, and the applause grew. "Really show them that they can do this if they really want to, we will be there with them."

Thomas continued speaking to the unchosen.

"We have a program for you. You will have your first counseling session today. Next week you may be ready, it may be next month, or maybe tomorrow, but when you are ready, you too will have the experience that we are about to share with these people now." He motioned with one hand and a well-dressed woman with a sharp angled haircut walked out of the wings.

"I'm going to ask my dear friend Anita to show you to your first session and I will be with you after this presentation." He motioned to the woman again. She, along with three brown polo-clad girls, ushered the disappointed people off-stage.

As they left, soft meditation music began and the first of three remaining people were brought to the edge of the now softly-lit pool.

Thomas got down on one knee in front of a bearded balding man in a wheelchair and looked him in the eye. The man only drooled his loose eyes darting around in his head. His withered legs were too still on the metal foot rests.

"You are going to have a fantastic experience, and as with all things unknown, you will feel a little afraid at first, but the fear will settle, and you will go into a beautiful place of healing and peace. Some who come out say they have seen the faces of loved ones who have passed. They come to help you, do as they say. Things are going to be wonderful for you now."

He unbuckled the safety belts holding the man upright in his chair and the man slumped over. Thomas held his shoulders to steady him as he slowly walked backward into the water, pulling the wheelchair and the catatonic man with him until they were waist deep. A man in a red polo collected the empty wheelchair. The man slipped into the water. Thomas cradled his neck, holding his head and shoulders above it.

"This man is a quadriplegic, but when he arises from this water he will come away clear, whole, washed of the crippling effect of his disease, washed of the memories of his life with his crippling disease. He will come out of this water and start a new life."

He took the man's head in his hands and pulled it under the water. Suddenly the water rolled and churned like a whirlpool and Oni released the man into the swirl, throwing his arms wide in the same embracing gesture with which he had started the presentation.

In what seemed like a long minute the man remained under water than then sprang from it gasping for air and threw his head back, water flying in an arc from his hair and beard. His eyes were wide as he re-acclimated himself to the light.

"Where am I?" he yelled as he stood with is his own two strong legs and walked out of the pool!

The crowd erupted in screams and applause. Jennifer looked around. Some people were crying, some were on their knees.

"Sir, you are now on the mend. Look at your feet, you are standing." The man looked down and screamed in disbelief. He threw his hands in the air and almost fell back into the pool out of elation. He started to bow but Thomas stopped him.
"Oh, no sir, that was not ME, that was the healing power of The Mend." He turned to his audience "YOU did that! The power of the LOVE in this room and of this man's own MIND healed him."

Thomas was silent until the audience was silent as well. He whispered. "Never let anyone tell you that it was Thomas Oni that made you whole." He gestured out of the pool and the man walked out, dripping. Anita was waiting with two enormous towels. She wrapped the first around the man and handed the second to Thomas.

"You are free now to walk to your new life waiting just off stage, you are free to walk through the rest of your life a healed man."

The Mend

The crowd roared as he slowly and hesitantly walked, then kicked up his heels and danced off stage flanked by two young men in brown polos.

Two bells softly chimed and on cue Jennifer's guide tapped her on the shoulder. "That means Greens are requested to begin their orientation." She whispered. "That's you. Follow me."

They stood and sidled down the row to the aisle.

"Ladies and gentlemen before we proceed, some of the newest members of our organization will be leaving us for service and learning opportunities. Let's say 'thank you' to them in advance."

Jennifer followed her guide to a side door to the sound of diminishing applause.

As the door closed, Oni knelt in front of a girl in a little pink wheelchair embedded with rhinestones. Her well-dressed parents waited just off stage. She heard him say in a stage whisper, "Princess, we are about to have a magical experience together."

Chapter Twelve

"There are two kinds of pride, both good and bad.
'Good pride' represents our dignity and self-respect.
'Bad pride' is the deadly sin of superiority that reeks
of conceit and arrogance."
-John C. Maxwell

"Exhilarating!" Thomas shouted as he walked through the iron doors to his personal sanctuary.

His "three wise men" whom he had recruited drunk in a honky-tonk in Bakersfield years before, stood at different positions in the room waiting for him. Stan, Mike and Forrester all looked healthy, strong and aware, far different from when he had fought them to join him. They were his disciples.

"I thought you said you would never do children!" The paunchy man, Stan, didn't meet Thomas's eyes when he made the statement. His bulbous face was flushed as it always was, but there was a deeper red, the color of anger.
The thin man, Mike, beside him held his breath. His eyes were wide in anticipation of the reply, he had been hoping for details of the experience.

"That kid didn't have anything. Drooling was her best talent. Did you see her face as she went under? She saw God!"

"She was a kid though, she had time…" Thomas was suddenly, violently, inches from the fat man's face.

"NOBODY HAS THAT KIND OF TIME!" Thomas bellowed. "Time to lie in a bed and stare into space? Time to have her green slimy nose and her filthy leaking ass wiped because she can't do it herself? Time to have tasteless goo pumped into her stomach because she can't eat?"

Thomas elbowed the sagging belly of the big guy at the word "eat" for emphasis.

"I did her the greatest favor. She is better off washed. Those parents are thrilled. They now have the daughter they always wanted. They have a future. That little girl has a future. …and it felt soooooo gooooood."

The thin man, who had been holding his breath, audibly gasped. Thomas's attention turned to him.

"Do you have something to say too? You're the reason she's here. Fuckin' pervert."

The thin man had a taste for young flesh. Thomas didn't share his vice but now he understood the concept.

It was Mike's shameful appetite that had brought the girl to Thomas's attention. Mike bought her from a brothel in the Philippines where she had lived all of her battered eight years.

Stan was grateful that Thomas had turned his attention from him. He was in no better shape to take Thomas on now than he had ever been.

He was also grateful that when the little girl had taken the first breath of her new life onstage that morning, her old life forgotten. She was now out of reach of Mike and every other predator she had been doomed to encounter. She was now safe with parents she did not recognize who could mold her life for the better.

Thomas remembered the day the parents of the little brain-damaged girl came to him, begging him to heal the twisted, pale child whose twitching eyes were all that moved in her unlucky body. At first, he had been reluctant, but then the thought of doing something he had never done before grew in his head.

In the years he had cultivated and led the movement, he had used his carefully-attained power to privately satisfy nearly every fantasy he had.

He had tested new experiences on women, men, teenagers and even a few animals and although they had satisfied him for a while nothing matched the pleasure he got when he washed someone new. He ached for Saturday mornings to feel the thrill of pushing them down, holding their head between his legs, feeling the spasms as they thrashed in the whirlpool, clinging desperately to the last moment of useless lives and then the exhilaration of release as a brand-new person came out clear.

That one glorious moment was brief for him and every time he wanted more. He loved that he could do it in front of thousands of people and they cheered him on!

But he had never washed a child until today. The pleasure was overwhelming.

He expected derision from Stan. He had lately begun to develop a dangerous conscience. He had not counted on disapproval from Mike.

"Did you put the wannabes in the dissuasion room?" He asked the third man, Forrester.

"Yes, Anita took them there. They have decided to embrace their disabilities."

"And their poverty? Anyone troublesome?" He liked that his second in command was standing at attention.

"No. All good sir. They all believe they've spoken with you."

The best thing about all three men being with him from the start, was the safety it afforded him. They could be implicated in anything he did so they made sure he was never implicated.

Today he wasn't sure it was enough. He had been watching the cameras he had ordered installed in Stan's room and lately he had seen a marked change

in his behavior. Porn, pills, pot and port weren't sedating him anymore. He spent his nights alone sitting in the dark, the red ember of his endless cigarettes the only indication that he was awake; some nights all night long.
He had recently lost weight. Thomas could sense his instability.

Insomnia can cause mental illness but Thomas didn't fear the man's approaching madness; he expected it. Stan had always been the weak link. Thomas had been thinking of scheduling a well-timed heart attack for him and he hoped the other two men would recognize his work and know that there was nothing Thomas wouldn't do to protect The Mend.

He had counted on their unshakeable loyalty and he had gotten it since he had saved them from their forlorn realities long ago in the bar, but now things seemed to be changing with one.

Thomas was ready. He expected it.

Even with the tremendous power and respect they now enjoyed as his inner circle, even with access to the finest things, and even though Thomas had made their families comfortable and their lives easy, he didn't trust any of them fully to have his back.

There was a reason he kept people at arm's length. He knew human nature, at least his own, and he knew that in their situation, he would be plotting to take the reigns too.

He was not going to make that easy for any of them.

He had installed hidden cameras initially to watch depraved Mike. The man was sloppy and he wanted to make sure he didn't accidentally expose his lustful crimes to those who stalked The Mend looking for reasons to destroy him. He had found that even Mike had a sick version of a conscience. Sometimes after his young prey had been programmed to forget and taken back to their dorm rooms, Mike would engage in self-flagellation. It worried him, so he had installed cameras in the rooms of the other two, wondering what he didn't know about them.

The fat man had his dark, silent weirdness but the third man, Forrester, was steadfast. His personal life was pure. He had never indulged in the wickedness of the others, only kept things neat.

He had joined The Mend in its beginning stages a raging alcoholic, but he no longer drank and spent his evenings reading, scribbling numbers in a ledger and talking with his daughter Ashlee, who was attending graduate school on a scholarship Thomas had provided.

Forrester recognized his service to Thomas and The Mend as a contract through which his daughter would never want for anything.

Experience in two wars had prepared him for anything he would witness. He wrote off the cruel things he heard and saw as an inevitable part of life. It was going to happen somewhere, to someone, at least here it had a good end result. Families were almost always overjoyed with Oni's results and no one was left to complain.

Forrester did as he was told and although he refused to kill, he cleaned up any mess that resulted from the others' carelessness. He was paid well and his daughter was back in his life. He had his work, only he knew how important it was and he had his books to tend.

The ledgers he kept worried Thomas a little. When he asked about it he had been shown a notebook full of nonsense numbers that Forrester explained away as "a complicated investment strategy". Numbers made no sense to Thomas. He dismissed it as voodoo accounting.

It was when he learned that computer programs were written using numeric codes that he became suspicious and had started to look for his own Ashlee for insurance. And now he had her.

The workshop where Anita had found her had proven to be a great way to get young people into The Mend. The operation required new energy. It was getting harder to fill the demand for The Wash.

He so loved The Wash.

Thomas wondered if he was enjoying it too much. The thin man had been right to hold his breath; things were getting chaotic. The messes were getting harder for Forrester to clean up and Thomas felt like things were getting beyond even his control.

Now he had washed a child. What if it had not worked? What if the little Filipino girl had drowned on her way up? And more importantly to him, how was he ever going to top that feeling?

Chapter Thirteen

Eric's phone rang and he was overjoyed to see it was Zack.

"Where are you?" He didn't waste a second on hello.

"I'm in California. I have to get Jen and Noah."

"Please wait until I get there. I want to help."

"I'm sorry Dad, you can't help me this time."

"Zack where did you get that kind of money?"

"Don't worry Dad, it's legal. When I can't sleep, I take freelance programming gigs, I earned all of it."

In the back of Eric's mind, he had known his son would never do anything illegal but it was comforting to be reassured, especially now that he knew of his lineage. "I'll be back, with Jen and Noah soon. Don't worry. I've got this."

"Zack, Thomas Oni. He doesn't do things the right way, do you understand? He makes his own rules about everything. All we've talked about, faces, right and wrong, none of it will work there. Please wait until I get to you."

He heard his own voice becoming shrill with panic. When he thought of harm coming to Zack, he couldn't control his feelings.

"I can't Dad, my phone is going off, stay there.

I'll be home soon."

The click reminded Eric of the cocking of a gun, Zack was behind this trigger and he hoped he wasn't unintentionally turning it on himself.

Zack looked around his hotel room. His lock-pick and alarm kits were laid out on the table, along with his tablet computer, a toy drone, a camouflage blanket, several clear-plastic tubes the size of needles, a bag of mixed computer components, a notebook, pencil, three vials of liquid, a box of syringes and a roll of duct tape. A week's worth of groceries stocked his mini-fridge. The front desk had been informed that he wanted no housekeeping for four days. The cable on the back of his television was cut to install his router.

He had everything he needed. He was ready.

Chapter Fourteen

"Success can be a trap of expectations."
-Dawn Howard

Jennifer threw herself across the giant bed in her new room and for a moment, relaxed. She was exhausted after three days of learning complicated new compositions, watching videos, painting portraits and participating in virtual reality sessions with her new guide, whose name she learned was Jackie.

She had been assigned a new purple badge that morning. The new tag seemed to disturb Jackie.

Jennifer understood her frustration, perhaps it was exhaustion. In the past three nights, Jackie had been called out of bed for some kind of emergency situation three times. When she came back from her meetings, she *said* she was fine, but Jennifer could hear her crying into her pillow.

Jackie brushed off Jennifer's one attempt to comfort her and had explained that although she had just turned 18, she had been a Blue for three years. She didn't understand how Jennifer had been with The Mend for three days and was already a purple. She was beginning to lose hope for a promotion.

Her lack of faith was short lived. Jennifer had gotten her purple badge only hours before Jackie got an orange one.

"I've been chosen! Finally!" She squealed. The apparently good news confused Jennifer who still had not been told what the colors meant, but it made Jackie so happy she bounced up and down on her bed. "You don't know what I've had to do for this! I'm an Orange!"

As she was celebrating there was a knock on the door. It was Thomas Oni's personal assistant Anita with the new badge. Jackie handed her blue badge to Anita, clipped the new orange one onto the collar of a crisp, new white polo and was immediately ushered away to her new status by a large man wearing a red badge.

Anita then presented Jennifer with her purple badge and ushered her to a new room. There was only one bed in the suite. Finally, she would have some time to herself!

The room was plush! A big plasma TV tucked between two bookcases filled one entire wall. The shelves were filled with interesting books, all best sellers, some of which Jennifer had been longing to read. She picked a few and put them on her nightstand for later and continued exploring.

The chocolate colored walls and creamy-soft gray couches were like the covers of the magazines her mother bought.

A white piano in the corner was in perfect tune. She walked her fingers over the keys on her way to the window.

The view of the ocean was magnificent. When she noticed that her room was on the cliff side, a flash of fear went through her. What if there was an earthquake? It *was* California! She quickly stepped back from the window, then laughed at her irrational Midwest fear.

Her bathroom was immense, much bigger than her living room at home. The waterfall shower was set into real stone. She flicked on the light switches, revealing a sun lamp in the shower as well.

She suddenly felt like she was being watched so she turned around. No one was there. She scanned the ceiling for cameras half expecting to see one but except for the sunlamp, the ceiling was smooth and clean. The room looked like it had just been remodeled.

Her fear subsided. Nonetheless she would wait until nightfall to shower. There was no phone, no computer and she had no roommate. The realization of her aloneness scared Jennifer more than the extravagance of the room, the possibility of earthquakes, or the possibility of being watched. She realized she had never actually been alone before. There was always her mother, or Zack and Noah, or her piano teacher or her dance team…

She felt like this was no longer a summer workshop. Now it was something …unknown. She ran to the door and grabbed the handle.

Locked! She was no longer a student. She was a prisoner!

Seconds later, as if on cue, Anita knocked on the door. Jennifer saw her through the peephole in the door.

"I can't let you in, the door is locked from the outside!" Jennifer screamed. She got no reply. The room was soundproof. Anita waited patiently while Jennifer looked around and finally noticed an intercom on the wall. She pressed the button. "It's locked, I can't get out!"

"Anita fumbled in her pocket for her electronic master key. "That's my fault." She said. "We keep these doors locked when no one is in them, otherwise kids go in there and wreck them! I must have locked it by habit. I'm sorry."

Jennifer flew out of the room and looked down the empty hallway wondering where all the other students were.

"You must have been so scared! Let me show you around. Now that you are a Purple, you get to see a whole different side of The Mend."

Jennifer was relieved to leave the beautiful room for a moment to escape her temporary fears. She followed Anita outside to a beautiful sculpted garden filled with flowers of every shape and size.

The smell of the flowers was intoxicating, but it was more than just floral, there was another smell under the sweet and it was not at all pleasant. She couldn't name it, but it made her uncomfortable.

Caretakers rolled people in wheelchairs, guided people on crutches and followed behind walkers over smoothly-paved pathways lined with handrails. They were all ages and varying degrees of disability. What struck Jennifer most was that each caretaker looked to a striking degree, like the person they were tending. Every attendant was wearing an orange badge. She looked around for Jackie but didn't see her.

"As you know, we run a charity for the disabled. You saw what Thomas can do the first day you were here, but outside of the flashiness of The Wash ceremony, a lot goes on behind the scenes.

All of these people are former students like you, who have graduated to orange level.

We call new people Greens. Green means 'go. When you are a Green and you finish the program, you either go home or you go toward another level.

Some decide to stay at the end of their Green program and continue to help. They become "True Blues". Those Blues that don't have families, live here and volunteer for service to The Mend night and day like a real family. They are the reason we are able to help so many.

The Mend

When someone graduates to Orange we send them to serve in one of our many branches in Europe, or to help us set up our fledgling operations in South America, like we did for your guide Jackie.

If they fit certain criteria and if they choose it, we partner them to someone to whom they can closely relate. You can see, sometimes they even look alike." Anita swept her hand across the garden like a game show hostess and smiled.

Jennifer was relieved; she had felt guilty for skipping blue and advancing to her purple badge, leaving her one friend behind now she was happy for Jackie, off adventuring South America. She made a mental note to ask Anita *why* she had skipped Blue but listened as Anita continued.

"Orange Menders who go through the partner program, like these people here, get to know their partners very well. We give them an unparalleled immersion experience designed by Thomas Oni himself.

We have special virtual reality rooms that mimic the brain wave patterns of their partners, to put them in the same frame of mind, so to speak. An Orange working with a quadriplegic will go into an isolation chamber where they can't feel their body. There they will see images of their partner's families, looking down to them, giving them a bath or feeding them so they know what it's like.

The Mend

They might choose to watch videos taken from a waist level point of view, which is eye level to someone in a wheelchair. They might choose to ride with their arms strapped to their sides in a wheelchair or wear a blindfold or earplugs to get the experience of paralysis, blindness, or deafness.

When one of our disabled people is ready for The Wash, their Orange member graduates to The Leadership Academy. Once that level is completed in our top-secret training center, they will be ready to lead the new centers I was just telling you about.

They leave here with great insight and are ready for new missions, but they will never forget what it's like to live with their partner's disabilities.

We think it builds understanding. When these people get to their new posts, they do great work in the world."

Anita pulled an entire head of petals from a wilting blood red rose, crushed them in her hand and held the petals to Jennifer's nose.

"They have such a unique smell."

Jennifer breathed in the scent of the rose. It was rich and full with a potency like no rose she had ever smelled, but for some reason it made her sad.

Anita smiled and looked at Jennifer to see if she was understanding and accepting her explanation. She seemed to be, so she continued.

"When you came to us as a Green we had no idea you had such splendid natural talents. We didn't know about your music. Your paintings are beautiful and so are you. That's why when you were promoted to Purple so quickly."

One mystery solved, so many more to decipher. Jennifer felt like there was something about The Mend that she wasn't grasping. It was more a feeling than a thought; like the under-smell of the garden, she instinctually didn't like it, but she didn't know what questions to ask to solve a puzzle she couldn't define.

Anita lifted the plunger on a device that looked like a giant French press coffee maker and dropped the petals into it as she continued.

"You got your grand room, free classes and all the amenities you now have, because we want you to stay as long as you like, have a good time and gain an understanding of what we do here so you can share our work through your art, with the world. You would be surprised how many famous people have gone through The Mend's fine arts program, just like you are now doing."

You can, of course, choose to leave at any time but we hope you'll enjoy your time enough here to stay. Take classes and relax, your only responsibility, as agreed when you signed up, will be to read to the severely disabled people we haven't partnered yet or if you like volunteer in other ways.

You may be asked to play a piece of music at dinnertime or paint something for one of our art auctions. It's your choice."

Jennifer smiled back at Anita. How could she have been so paranoid? This place was doing amazing work. She was embarrassed that she thought she was being locked up and she was embarrassed that she felt so suspicious of everything she had just seen. It was all perfect. Maybe she was just a bit homesick.

"Can I see my friend Noah?" she asked.
Anita froze in place for a fraction of a second. "You have a friend here?"
Maybe it was leftover paranoia, but it seemed Anita's face flashed past surprise to annoyance for a moment.
"His name is Noah Samuels. He got here the same day I did,"
"I will try to find him for you." Anita tapped his name into a tablet she pulled from inside her jacket.
"Noah Samuels… has chosen the security officer program. He's already signed on to become part of the organization. He'll start as an usher. You'll probably see him at the next Wash ceremony on Saturday."

Jennifer breathed a sigh of relief. The creepy feeling was going away. She was beginning to feel proud that she had found such an institute, or rather that Zack had found it for her.

She paid close attention in her art class that afternoon. She chose 'One Hour as a Blind Person' for her Disability Session and received drops in her eyes that made her temporarily completely blind.

Without her eyes, she challenged herself to play Boccherini's Minuet, for the disabled residents. She learned that they were called "Provisees" at dinnertime.

She had no way of knowing that Thomas Oni visited and watched her performance. On the way back to her room after dinner, she could not see the many "Authorized Personnel Only" signs in her wing of the unit, and that night she slept deeply in her soundproof suite.

She slept fitfully and dreamt of rotting flowers.

She would awaken grateful for her eyes in the morning light.

Chapter Fifteen

"New technology is not good or evil in and of itself.
It's all about how people choose to use it."
-David Wong

Zack switched off his laptop and wondered what Jennifer was doing just as her head was hitting her pillow. Although it was late in the night, his day was just beginning.

He had already hacked into the county auditor's building permit database and had studied every structure on the compound. It confused him. It read like unfinished video game programming.

The aerial view he compared the blueprint to showed that were several unexplained spaces, none of which had a permit attached to them. He would need to get inside or at least nearer to access the closed network, fill in the blanks and hack the cameras to find out which room she was in. He would try to find and brief Noah first; he might need his help.

Getting close enough to get access was a conundrum of its own. The stone wall, wire fences, dogs, and wi-fi blackout zones surrounded the heavily guarded compound. Several signs told him no unauthorized phones or electronic equipment of any kind were allowed through the steel gates. He had slipped in with a deliver van that was now parked in an odd place just outside one of the rear gates.

Zack stood in the one area he had found between oscillating cameras.
He crawled into some bushes, duct taped a disposable phone to the little remote-control drone and sent the device up to look for a wi-fi hotspot. He watched the drone for the light he had programmed to turn on when it found a signal and hoped he would be the only one to see it.

He didn't have to wait long. He lowered the little plane slowly to the ground and wrapped himself in the camouflage blanket and went to where it landed. He clicked on his tablet. To keep its glow from being seen, he kept the blanket over himself as he had done so many times as a child to read and to keep his dad from noticing that he didn't sleep.

The signal was strong. He ran the program he had written, opened several tabs and found passwords for the network. He looked for all independent computers and was surprised to find that some were being used in dorms on smart phones, against the rules.

He stared at them for a few moments to see if his hack had been detected. One by one, he ruled out useless devices and concentrated on getting into the computer that controlled the security cameras.

There were more than he had expected. First, he stop-screened the ones at the front and back gates, neither Noah nor Jennifer would have any reasons to be there. Then he blocked out the administrative buildings. After hours, no one would be there either… but wait…someone was there.

He was about to disregard that area when he saw a reflection of light. Following a hunch, he decided to hide that camera from the security feed. Whoever had placed that camera had a private feed. It was not on the network.

He took a screen shot and put it on a loop so whoever was monitoring it would see only the empty office.

He watched three people crouch and stay crouched behind some antiquated desktop computers. He knew from their posture they were removing the backs of some of them.

Whatever they took out or put in didn't take long, and soon the three were sneaking out of the building.

Zack took the loop off the feed and looked for them on the other cameras. They seemed to have disappeared but he noticed the numbers that denoted the passage of time on some of the feeds were not moving. Whoever had hacked the other cameras had done just what he had done. He followed the progress of the still numbers from camera to camera until he saw which exit the burglars would be coming out of. He sheathed his tablet, tossed it into his backpack with the blanket and drone, and made his way to where he predicted they would exit.

He reached them just as they were getting into the oddly parked van. He didn't bother running the van's plates, he knew that whoever had hacked the cameras was smart enough not to use a van registered to themselves.

He wondered why the van wasn't leaving and crept close to see if he could hear their conversation.

"Get in the car..." a slender woman holding a gun to his back suddenly whispered behind him. "and don't speak."

Zack tried to obey. He had read about staring down the barrel of a gun but until he felt one against his skin, he didn't realize how debilitating it was. He couldn't move.

He didn't have to. Someone opened the van's side door and the woman pushed him inside. The three from the camera were waiting.

The woman who pushed him inside got in the driver's seat and the strangely silent vehicle left the lot. Its lights remained off.

"What the hell were you doing outside kid? Apparently, you don't know what they do to runaways!" The woman with the gun snapped at him and tucked the weapon into its holster. She looked him up and down as if she was checking for damage.

"I wasn't trying to get out, I was trying to get in."

"Then apparently, you don't know what they do to intruders either! That place is not safe, you don't want anything to do with it." Her voice was serious and short.

"I know. My friends are in there. I have to get in to get them out. They don't know what's happening in there." He didn't know why he was still whispering.

"What do *you* think is happening in there?" asked a man asked from the back seat.

Zack turned to look at the man who was sitting beside another woman in the dark. He couldn't make out their faces. He decided he had said too much and shut his mouth.

"What do you know about The Mend kid?"

Zack remained silent.

"Who is this guy?" the driver asked.

Zack and the woman sat silently figuring out what they wanted to do with each other.

Eventually they pulled into an outdoor storage lot and the women went to unlock and open the gate leaving him alone with the men.

"You're in way over your heads." He finally said to the men who had resigned themselves to just sit quietly and wait him out.

"Your bugs have probably already been found. I hope there were no fingerprints on them." The two looked at each other.

With the last sentence, Zack had been fishing. He had caught what he hoped for. He motioned to the women who were waving them through the open gate and locking it behind them.

"Which one of them is Kelsea Stone?"

Chapter Sixteen

"Human behavior flows from three main sources: desire, emotion, and knowledge." - Plato

Kelsea Stone had been trying for years to prove that Thomas Oni was Wayne Walters. She had also worked hard to get her little sister's cold case reopened and ruled a murder. Wayne/Thomas Oni was her prime suspect. His sudden disappearance had convinced her of his guilt.

She remembered exactly the moment she had happened upon an interview with him on a national talk show. His hair was different but his face and voice were just the same. She was floored to see that he was famous. She contacted the police but her report was disregarded and she was viewed as a celebrity stalker.

Since then she had made several attempts to speak to him and had set up a website called, "How Do You Mend a Murder" devoted to her pursuit of justice for her sister. But Oni filed suit to have it taken down and filed a restraining order against her.

She was jailed when, after a highly publicized break-in at his house, her fingerprints were found on a flashlight in his study.

She had never been there.

She served 6 months in jail. Since then, her entire life had become about bringing him to justice.

It was from an FBI archive of her blog that Zack had attained a lot of his information about Oni. He was eager to talk to her.

He didn't have to wait long. He followed the four into a 30-foot RV hidden under a blue tarp in the full storage lot.

They emptied his backpack onto the table. A pair of night vision glasses fell to the floor.

"This how you found us?" one of the men asked as he placed it on the table with the rest of the equipment.

"I found you by accident and you should be glad I did. You missed a camera. If I hadn't turned it off, they would have had lots of footage of all of you to take to the police."

"Thanks." Kelsea smiled at him. "But they would never use legal means to get rid of us. If they caught us, we would be dead.   We *were* lucky you were there. Who are you?"

"I told you, I have friends in The Mend that I'm trying to break out."

"What's your name?"

He decided to trust her. "Zack Rubin."

"Are your friends Provisees?"

"I don't know, they've only been there a week and I haven't talked to them, that's part of the problem, no one can reach them. What's a Provisee?"

142

"It's their word for a sick or disabled person who is scheduled to be mended. Are you here alone?"

"I am, and I'm on your side, I assure you. Please tell me more."

Kelsea looked at one of the men who was picking through all of Zack's belongings. He handed her his school ID. She checked the name on it. The overexposed photo was partially obscured by an official seal. Still, he looked familiar.

"How did you know my name?"
"I read your blog."
"Why so much equipment, you can't just ask your friends to come out?"
"I can't reach them, they gave up their phones and computers. It's just as well. Oni killed their parents, if I alert him, he might kill them too."
"What else do you know? Tell us everything."

Zack related what he had read about Oni on the FBI database, Kelsea looked visibly relieved when Zack told her he knew Thomas Oni was Wayne Walters. He did not tell her about the suspected genetic relationship he had to Oni, only that his two best friends were inside and he had made it his mission to get them out.
If that meant shutting down the Mend, he was in league with Kelsea and her crew. He showed her the codes he uploaded to unlock the security computers, and suddenly, she trusted him too.

"We've been trying for years to decode the camera-embedded badge system they use to classify members. They keep their inner workings to a very tight group. Maybe you can help with that."

"If your friends are new, they probably wear green or yellow badges. We have decoded the audio on those."

One of the men spoke up. "They are probably Greens. We know where they sleep, we can guide you to them."

The other woman looked puzzled, "I thought membership was frozen. How did they get in?"

"They filled out an application for a summer workshop and were gone the next day." Zack explained.

Kelsea said she had never heard of such a program, she was suspicious again and Zack was beginning to feel angry at himself for not stopping them. He had found The Mend and given it his two best friends. "What's a Green?"

Kelsea pulled out a tablet computer and sketched out a chart. The other three went to unload the van as she explained. "Almost everyone starts out as a Yellow or a Green."

"Let's start from the bottom. Most members are Yellows. They are the curious, the new folks, friends of members, and long-term members who have no real value to the organization. Wayne allows them to attend Saturday services and they get to call themselves members for the sake of their small but loyal donations. Yellows are harmless and they don't know anything.

Promising Yellows can move up in the organization. The Mend uses a series of cameras and virtual reality games to watch members and find out where they fit. If someone is not open to suggestion, and not particularly bright, they go home.

Your friends are probably Greens. Greens are either smart or really gullible. They get into programs and live at The Mend while they decide what to do with them."

Kelsea pointed to a series of dorm rooms not too deep into the compound, close to the front of the building. The Greens that are marginally smart but unusually obedient become 'Browns'… security guards, custodians, ushers, and maintenance. They are faithful, loyal and employed." Kelsea showed Zack points on a map where browns might be located.

"But if someone is young, smart, malleable AND they fit a certain dependency profile, they bring them into the organization as Blues. They're the worker bees.

Kelsea cleared her throat, assessed Zack's expression to see if he was with her and continued.

"If a Blue is not particularly attractive they might work behind the scenes making Oni brand perfume, or in production on their elaborate Saturday Service.

Cute and personable Blues work in Mend Organic Markets and AmMend Healing Spas.

They use attractive Blues to recruit new members, collect donations, and as influencers to promote them online.

Really attractive Blues that are not too bright are there just to make the right people happy, if you know what I mean..."

Zack didn't. He clicked through blog pages uploaded by Blues showing smiling people doing useful work. They all looked like they were having a good time. He hoped Jennifer and Noah were as well.

Kelsea saw the far-away look in his eyes and realized he was young and inexperienced so she moved on.

"Blues do as they are told because they are very eager to become Purples. They will do almost anything they are asked and that makes them a commodity. They don't promote them unless they have a really good reason. Blues stay Blues as long as they are productive.

They can work their way up but if they cause problems they are sent 'to mission' as an Orange and Zack..."

Kelsea held the tablet computer against her chest and away from Zack's eyes for a moment.

"Once Oranges go away, they don't ever come back. Sometimes an Orange becomes a partner to a Provisee before being sent to mission, but that's another long story."

Kelsea put the computer back on the table of the dimly lit RV.

"Purples are the lucky ones. They usually have talents or exceptional abilities. They are treated especially well and are groomed to become ambassadors for the movement.

The Mend sometimes clears the path for them to become famous and powerful. That's why Blues work so hard to be Purples. You've seen Purples on television and in movies. I'll bet you own some of their music.

If Purples do well and become influential, they become Golds. Golds are the Gods of the Mend. They are what everyone aspires to. Millionaires. Billionaires."

The three others had finished unloading the van and were now sitting in on the instructional session.

Kelsea elaborated. "Some very wealthy people come in at the top as Golds. They are the superstars, dignitaries and politicians. Their membership is top-secret. The Mend operates a resort island just for them. Willing Blues live there reserved for their pleasure. It's the way Blues become Purples if they have no talent. You've probably seen some of *them* on television too. I'm sure you would know the ones, they are talentless, but somehow famous."

Zack sat very still, committing to memory everything Kelsea was telling him. She wasn't finished. Her face suddenly got serious.

"Now, let me warn you about Reds. Red badges are dreadfully worrisome. They are merciless mercenaries." Her face was very pale and her eyes stared into his. "We call them Redmen. If you see a Redman, you are in big trouble, probably already on your way to dead. They are exceptionally dangerous. They are smart and ruthless, they're true believers and they are *very* well paid.

Jarrod, one of two men sitting across from Zack, took over.
"Redmen are the enforcers of the movement: the cleaners, the strong arms, those that are willing to throw themselves on a grenade for The Mend. They keep the Golds, the important Purples and Oni untouchable."

"They usually don't even wear badges unless they are posted in high security sections of compound. They can be identified by members who know about them by barely noticeable red replacement buttons on their shirts. That's why if you see one, it's too late to run. With a red badge or button, one can go anywhere and do anything on the compound. We are working to get our hands on one but so far, no luck."
"Have you tried a remote cloning program? You just have to be close to one, you don't have to have it."

Jarrod looked gobsmacked. The answer was so simple only a (very intelligent) child could think of it.

Zack sighed, they were a clever group, but he wasn't sure they were up to the plan he had ready.

148

"That fills in some missing pieces, but you sort of glossed over Orange. It seems important. How does one become an Orange?"

"Oranges are the most unfortunate but they think it's a great honor. They are told that after immersion training, which is basically deep-mind hypnotism, they will be leading a team to start a new program in a foreign country. In reality, their brains are altered with lasers and their faces are altered with surgery. They use them as replacements for Provisees. Do you know what they do to Provisees?"

Kelsea hesitated at the second question unsure if she should tell him the story or how much he already knew.

"I've read they heal them in some sort of hyper-genetic miracle water. What do you mean replace Provisees? Why would they want to create disabled people after they have…?" Zack's mind had not wanted to accept what it knew, but it was suddenly too obvious to ignore.

"They drown them." Jarrod spoke up. "Oni kills them right in front of a thousand screaming fans and replaces them with Oranges that look just like them."

Jarrod anticipated more of a reaction from Zack than he got. The kid sat completely frozen, even his eyes were still. He hesitated but continued.
"The compound was built on an old graveyard for a reason. They shred and mulch the dead bodies of the

Provisees along with paper and kitchen waste and feed them to their prize-winning flowers and produce."

He paused again expecting a reaction from Zack that still wasn't there. "If anyone tests the soil, which they won't, because Oni owns the law, they can just say the human DNA is from the old graveyard."

The four conspirators stared at the young man who sat perfectly, robotically still, for over a minute before he spoke.

"I know Kelsea and Jarrod's story, but who are you?" Zack said to the other couple.

"My name is Ada, and this is my husband Patrick. Thomas Oni mended our son, Charlie." The small woman started, quivered and stopped to catch her breath. Patrick caressed her shoulder.

"He had cerebral palsy. He was 24, bright and funny and we just wanted the best that life could offer him. Oni promised him a cure, a fresh start. He charged us a $250,000 'donation'. We gladly sold everything we had for Charlie and moved into this Winnebago."

"He was so happy to go. He was there for a month before we were invited to the ceremony. He was really glad to see us but so excited to go into 'The Wash', which is what they call their healing ceremony. It was an incredible experience full of showmanship and music and excited people. We were overjoyed when Charlie stood up and walked for the first time. We just couldn't believe our eyes. With good reason of course.

When he came home, he looked and acted different but they said he would. He could immediately walk and talk but he wasn't bright and happy anymore. He just wandered around in a stupor for a long time like a bored 8-year-old. Then he started to have nightmares and he would wake up and he didn't know us."

Patrick took over when tears started to run down Ada's face.
"One afternoon, we took him to the Y to go swimming, he loved swimming, but out of the blue he was terrified of the water, he wouldn't go in. We thought maybe he subconsciously thought that being in the water would make him the way he was before.

That's when we noticed his c-shaped birthmark, the one that convinced us to name him Charlie, was gone, as well as a little scar he got from a feeding tube when he was a teenager. He wasn't our son at all! We took him to an aftercare doctor provided free of charge by The Mend who did a DNA test on him and it came back that he was indeed our son, they showed us the paperwork. But Ada and I were not convinced. We took some of his hair out of his hairbrush and we had a friend, who is a research fellow at Washington State, do the DNA test and it showed the truth. He wasn't related to us at all."

Patrick took a deep breath and Ada, newly composed, continued in his place.

"No one believed us. Charlie absolutely refused to submit to another test."

"Then the replacement Charlie suddenly got very sick and died. The Mend swooped in and cremated him immediately; apparently it was part of the small print of the contract we both signed. Then it was all over…they took our only son. Twice"

Zack listened to the story and tried to garner a timeline from what he was told. When a donation is given, the disabled person enters The Mend and a partner is assigned to them. That partner is programmed and surgically altered to look and feel like them. Four weeks later the disabled person is 'Washed' and their replacement goes home with the family as them. The replacement is sent home disoriented and without any memories but able to walk and talk.

Just four weeks from entering the compound to leaving as a different person. Assuming the worst-case scenario, one of his friends would be chosen as an "Orange", he had two weeks to get Noah and Jennifer out.

"What about the families of the replacements?" Surely someone would file a missing person's report. He asked, while his head was running through the logic of the Mend process.

The families of the Mended couldn't file wrongful death suits. Most of them have no families, also, with no body, there is no crime.

Zack was trying to decide if the literal "kill switch" was implanted in the replacement before they left The Mend or when they submitted to a DNA test. Replacements had to have friends who would miss them, and if the last place they were all seen was The Mend, that was grounds for a federal investigation. Thomas Oni couldn't pay off the FBI.

Jarrod answered. "They choose people who have been in the foster system, who have no family, sometimes street people. In some cases, if they need the type, they choose people with no siblings and only one parent, but only if they have no extended family."

"The ones with one parent, they just kill the parent." Zack said. Now he knew why Noah's dad and Jennifer's mom had died.

"They choose people with elderly or ailing parents if they can, but yes. If they need that face or body type badly enough, they kill them." Kelsea sighed and laid back against the seat. Telling the story was depressing her.

"How do you know these things?" Zack asked, "It seems a lot of inside information for four people whose have never been members." So far, their only connection to the Mend was a dead boy who had cerebral palsy and a limited vocabulary.

Kelsea turned to a reel to reel tape deck and flipped a switch.

"She's got to be 5 feet six and have blond hair."

"Like this one?"

"A little heavier."

"What about her?"

"What does her social media look like?"

"Like she's a bookworm with 11 followers."

"She will do."

This is audio from people who have no badges, the innermost circle, the three wise men. Their mistake was leaving a box of badges within earshot.

"You hacked the badges, that will make things easier." Zack was impressed, these people showed promise as accomplices.

Kelsea nodded. "Just the audio, but maybe you can help with the video part, as I've said, every badge has a camera." She looked him in the eye for a second, still doubting his place in the group. They knew nothing about him and they were telling him secrets. What if he had been planted outside The Mend to be captured by them?

"Tell me about your friends."

"Noah gets told he looks familiar a lot, he could probably fit the mold for a lot of guys. He lives with his dad. His dad had lung cancer. He overdosed on pain meds this week." Zack now knew without a doubt, it was no accident.

"Jennifer is gorgeous and she was close to her mother. She was healthy and they were close. She died in a car crash, this week." Zack liked Debbie, he would miss her.

"Your friend Noah is exactly what they look for. But Jennifer, does she have an unusual ability or is she just beautiful?"

"Both. She's a pianist and she's shown some art at galleries, some online." He reached for his tablet. Jarrod pushed it toward him and he quickly maneuvered through screens to sign into a proxy and showed them her blog. "She's too smart to be taken in by this."

"That's worrisome." Kelsea's brow wrinkled in concern, both over the fact that it was so easy for the boy to get in and to a proxy network so quickly on her wi-fi, and for his friends. "If she isn't loyal, she'll be in danger."

"I have to get them out of there." Zack said. "I'm the reason they are there."

"It's not going to be easy, their security would be a match for the Secret Service. We have a plan to shut down the entire Mend. The wireless adaptors we put in last night were the first step."

"Wireless adaptors? Seriously? They have already found and disabled them I'm sure. I think you need my help, and I need your help finding my friends."

"Finding them is now part of the plan, but we can use all the help we can get."

The rest of the night was spent brainstorming and strategizing.

As the two couples slept well into the next day, Zack sorted his computer components and built a tiny arsenal of weapons.

He was grateful for his insomnia. Now that time had become his enemy, every second counted.

Chapter Seventeen

Eric asked for ginger ale when the flight attendant came by.

He took his handful of afternoon pills and continued scribbling in his journal. It was the 18th and final book in a series of daily memoirs he had started the day Zack was born. He wrote these words:

"Zack, I'm sorry that you are reading this now, but I will be even sorrier if you never get the opportunity. If you are reading this, I have succeeded in extracting you from a treacherous situation. You are the most important thing in my life and I want you to appreciate each new day you have left in yours.

As I look out at the sun above the clouds, on my way to you, I am in awe. This world is full of terrible things, but the beauty everywhere in the world makes them insignificant by comparison. Enjoy the beauty Zack. See the intricacies of a leaf, listen to the sound of wind chimes, savor the taste of new spices, feel the waves of the ocean against your legs, smell the mossy earth of a forest in summer. I'll be there in spirit, Zack, and if I'm very lucky in body too. I'm already on my way."

He put the journal in a manila envelope he had brought and addressed it to himself at his home. If he got there first, Zack would never know it existed, but if he didn't, he wanted the boy to know how much he cared.

Chapter Eighteen

"The true beauty of music is that it connects people.
It carries a message, and we, the musicians,
are the messengers."
–Roy Ayers

Jennifer looked for Noah everywhere but in the expansive compound with her strict schedule, a chance encounter was possible but unlikely. The reunion Anita had promised had never happened. She wondered if it would.

"He is in an intensive training program." had been the simple answer to her questions, but in the three weeks she had been there, she had visited almost every section of the compound.

She had tried a few times to ditch her ubiquitous guides in order to explore… unsuccessfully.

They would take her almost anywhere she wanted to go with three exceptions.

There was the medical wing in which highly contagious Provisees stayed. Until they were mended and able to safely rejoin people, that area was out of bounds to everyone but doctors.

Only two other areas were forbidden to her purple badge, one was the mechanical sub-basement that was located directly under the meeting theater, and the other was Thomas Oni's private sanctuary.

She had seen only three other men enter that area, and she never saw them exit. She was sure there was a private exit elsewhere. She assumed it was in the theater as it was the only door from which she had ever seen Oni exit and not return.

She and her guides were granted access to the echoing meeting hall in order to practice for a performance that was a week away. She was shown her stage marks and cues and was allowed to play the piano to get a feel for the keys and pedals. It was a tedious process waiting for the equipment cues and for the other performers to be instructed. She occupied herself with the piano.

She was absentmindedly tapping out the notes to The Flower Duet, from Lakmé, when Thomas Oni appeared behind her out of nowhere.

"That's from my favorite opera." He said the words so quietly it was almost a whisper. The bright lights behind him made seeing his face difficult for a moment. She had never been this close to him before. He looked older than he did on stage and more familiar.

"I learned it for my best friend, he loves it too." She missed Zack; she had not been away from him for more than a few days since kindergarten. It had now been three weeks. She wondered if he missed her too.

She played it again, this time with both hands and her whole heart.

Oni stepped out from in front of the lights to watch her play. He softly hummed along, his eyes closed through the entire piece and when she finished he asked her friend's name.

"Zack," she said. Noticing he wanted more information, she added, "Rubin. Zack Rubin." She thought about how Noah would make fun of the way she said it in such a "Bond. James Bond" fashion and smiled as if he just had, Oni nodded serenely but a troubled look passed across his face.

"I'd like you to play that on Saturday instead." He spun on his heel and disappeared in the direction from which he had come without another word.

She suddenly didn't want to know where the other door to his part of the compound was located. He left her with the creeps.

Although she would attend practice all week, he never showed up again.

Her mind went back to Zack and then to the mystery of Noah.

She would make it a project to find him tomorrow.

Coincidentally Eric, who had just arrived, heard the notes to The Flower Duet coming from the theater and also thought of Zack as he entered the front doors of The Mend.

He had his medical files under his arm and he dropped them on purpose as the man who had picked him up from the airport manually started to guide him away from the direction of the music.

Papers went in every direction, scattering the meticulously organized files like shuffled cards on the floor. It bought him time to look around.

"I'm sorry sir, sit down here and we will put this back together." The man set about gathering and organizing the papers and Eric studied his surroundings, observing people who were coming and going, hoping to find his son. The man then went to get a wheelchair as Eric put the last of the papers back in order. He promised to be right back and closed and locked the door behind him.

"Hey Mr. Rubin!" Noah, dressed in a security guard uniform was walking toward him.

"Hey kid, you're looking fancy! Got a job huh?" Eric looked over the boy and was grateful to see that he was alive, happy and healthy.

"I'm doing my mandatory volunteer time as a security guard. Everybody wants to bring a phone or a camera in here and it's my job to keep them out."

"Why no cameras?"

"Privacy. Sort of a 'religious freedom' thing." Noah made air quotes and grinned a sideways grin.

"We get a lot of celebrities and important people here and I guess they don't want their photos all over the Internet."

"Sure, I get that. Have you seen a lot of celebrities?"

"Not so far, but we are doing a Wash ceremony this Saturday so they will probably be here for that, that's a big thing."

"Oh, a Wash Ceremony. That's a big deal huh?" He didn't tell the boy he was here to sign up for one.

"Oh yeah, it's a big healing event. This week 10 Provisees are going to be washed. In the history of The Mend, the most they have ever done in one day is five."

"Wow, that *is* big! Hey, have you seen Zack or Jennifer?"

"No, I hear Jennifer is performing this weekend, but I didn't even know Zack was here!"

That answered Eric's question. Zack had not found a way to join. He hoped he had not just given away anything that might endanger any of them.

"Oh no, he came with me. He must be outside." He motioned to the door hoping for what Noah would do next.

"I'll get him!" Noah's face brightened at the thought of seeing his best friend. He disappeared out the front door just as Eric's guide came back to usher him into the intake office for prospective Provisees.

Zack stared at a 46-inch screen upon which 280 images simultaneously changed every four seconds.

After trying unsuccessfully to hack the camera badges for video, he gave up in favor of a better idea. He had spent much of the previous night gluing micro-transmitters onto feeder bugs he bought at a pet store. Some had escaped. He noticed two crickets resting on the screen.

It was a project he had done alone while the others slept. He had no fear of bugs, but understood some people did.

As he was pouring the buckets of bugs over the stone walls that were closest to the buildings, he felt a little bad for the kids who would encounter the fat feeder roaches, and he felt bad for the roaches and crickets too. No doubt they would breed and then they and their progeny would be exterminated. (The moths would live but only their short life cycle, which was coming to an end anyway.)

He hoped the little cameras would have done their job and that he was back in Ohio before any of the deaths occurred.

Many of the 280 spots on the screen were gray or completely blank as the microscopic cameras on the bugs were now lost or pointed into the cracks and crevices into which bugs crawl.

He had been watching for two hours when he jumped to attention. Jennifer was playing piano in the top-right corner upside down. He stopped that photo, rotated it and maximized it on the screen.

That bug was on the ceiling of the auditorium. He located and connected to her badge. The audio was clear. She was playing his favorite song.

He smiled, something he seldom did without her, and tried to zoom in, but the electronic stimulus of the change caused the bug or at least the tiny camera attached to it, to fall to the floor. It remained motionless. If the camera had been dislodged it would just look like a piece of an earring to anyone that might have noticed it at all.

He glanced again at the whole screen hoping for a glimpse of her from a different direction and was horrified to see on another bug, his DAD walking through the front doors of The Mend.

He blew that image up to size and tried to get better audio. His dad wasn't wearing a badge and the man he was speaking with wasn't either. There was Noah and he had a badge, but he was leaving!

He had to stop himself from crying out and waking the others when he saw Eric go through the intake door. He watched the screen carefully as minutes turned into half an hour and his dad did not come back out. It meant he was not rejected for the program, it meant he would be scheduled to be Mended.

He searched the network for signs that any of the hundreds of insects he had fitted with his own design for low intensity light-powered cameras, had found their way into the inner offices, and for one second, he found a bit of hope. One had. The hole into which it had crawled did not allow for a visual but Zack faintly heard the sound of his father's voice. He touched the red dot to record the conversation.

His hope was crushed when only a few audible words stood out in the faint audio he could receive. He backed up the recording and played it again, enhancing it for clarity.

"Cancer…. weeks." Why had he not been told?

Everything must now be changed. Instead of two, there were three to be saved before they rendered The Mend to oblivion.

He set the cameras to recognize the frequency of his father's voice. He typed in "voice activate, record all" to review later and went to find Kelsea.

She was flying between two dust-covered RVs checking the strength of a body harness she had connected to almost invisible wires. She clicked a remote in her hand and descended silently to the ground, as his panicked words reached her ears.

"We have to move earlier." He was shaking and seemed distraught so she reached out to put her hand on his shoulder. He froze, rocking slightly on the balls of his feet.

"Stop! If you are going to be part of this, you have to learn to act like a regular person. Regular people get touched when they are upset."

Zack steeled himself through the overwhelming sensation of a near stranger's human electricity on his skin. He un-paralyzed his facial muscles by force of will and managed to smile.

"Well done. Now tell me, what's the matter?" Kelsea withdrew her hand and stepped back to give the kid some relief.

"Three things. One, both of my friends will be at the ceremony tomorrow. Two, so will my father. And three, he's asking to be mended!"

"This really does mess things up. They are all in deep trouble if anything goes wrong, so we have to make sure everything goes right."

"It has to." he confirmed, "and it will."

Chapter Nineteen

"There are weapons that are simply thoughts. For the record, prejudices can kill and suspicion can destroy."
-Rod Serling

Thomas paced the floor of his expansive office in front of his three men. He was agitated and none of them knew why.

He looked to Mike first. "Find the person responsible for the 'Club Mend' recruitment forum and get them out of this world. None of those kids were vetted.

Put the un-partnered ones we got from that failure in the mix too. Do what you want with them but get rid of them all."

He knew the thin man was ready for a pervert-fix. Several young people already marked for death would allow him to act on his sickest impulses, relieve his stress and hopefully, help him stay loyal.

All three men were silent. When Thomas was in this kind of mood, talking to him only made it worse.

He turned to Stan who was trying to hide a horrified expression. "There is a new Provisee. His name is Eric Rubin. I want a replacement found for him TODAY. He is going in The Wash tomorrow.

Don't tell me it can't be done. You just have to find someone who looks similar to him from a distance, he's an old man on a big stage. Search the missions."

He turned to Forrester. "I want you to put all security on the lookout for *this* kid."
He held up a copy of a framed photo of Zack and Eric that Eric kept on his mantel.
"He is connected to one of the unvetted kids AND to the Provisee. He is not here, which means he is coming. My researchers tell me he's a little genius and he's up to something. I can feel it."

Thomas's research team didn't mess around when it came to Provisees. They knew everything about Eric Rubin, including the capabilities of his only son. It was no coincidence that Jennifer had mentioned his name the same day his father showed up to be processed for Mending. When the researcher could not locate the boy, who was coincidentally born on the day his sister died, nine months after he had left Cleveland, Thomas put the pieces together. The boy was dangerous and he was near.

Thomas picked up a humanitarian award he had been given by a local charity and threw it against the wall, shattering the glass.

The fat man, winced and almost imperceptibly began to tremble.

Thomas didn't look in his direction but back to Forrester.

"You personally keep your eyes on Jennifer Wilson at all times He will be coming for her. Don't let her know you're watching but don't let her out of your sight for even a second. From this point on, she is treasure."

He knew the word would evoke a feeling of value for the girl whom Forrester would find was a stranger-twin to his daughter, Ashlee.

Zack Rubin would not get the queen of his chessboard. He would get nothing.

Thomas had a bad feeling about the kid from the moment the pretty little pianist had said his name.

Something in the way she had played and had looked so confident at the thought of him, told him that even though they had taken care of her one remaining family member, this boy would come for her. Love always complicates things.

He put a team of researchers on the kid, and what they reported alerted him to the threat. The kid was a prodigy with resources. He had bought a same day ticket to Los Angeles and was registered at an expensive hotel, the closest one, minutes from The Mend. No one had seen the kid enter or leave his room in days.

The Mend

Then his father showed up, asking to be mended. It meant the boy and his father were up to something. He had not simply come and asked for the girl, which meant he intended to do more than fetch her.

His team had connected more dots and identified Zack as a respected hacker and an expert level gamer, someone who thinks three moves ahead. Thomas would just have to think four moves ahead.

They had already found evidence of the boy's intrusion into some vulnerable camera relays and two planted wi-fi repeaters.

His team had disabled the kid's spying devices and all camera badges just to be safe. A sweep by his best man had shown no more bugs.

The kid was coming for the girl. He would make her available but keep her where he controlled the escape route. She would be a pretty trap and an insurance policy.

He didn't know yet how the boy's father factored in, but if he was a mole he had not given up his secrets despite enhanced questioning. He been rendered ineffective by sedation. He lay unconscious in the infirmary until Thomas had time to question him himself.

Moving up his Mending would put the kid on the defensive. He would show himself and he would be deactivated.

Ridding the compound of everyone that had come in with the girl would remove any last trace of her existence there. He would once again have a clean situation, Forrester would be duly warned of future dangers, and life would go on.

Thomas was used to intrusion. It wasn't the first time The Mend had been threatened, there were a few nagging loose-ends he intended to tie up soon. This minor mess was just practice for the next one.

Thomas felt good about putting Forrester on the girl. He would keep her safe and get the message. There was no one he couldn't Mend.

Thomas hated that he couldn't read his top-security officer, sometimes he felt he was another loose end. Like Stan and the pesky sister of a girl in Pittsburg he barely remembered.

None of the methods he had learned or developed had prepared him for the man's defenses. He did know that he had only one weakness but Thomas was not sure what would happen if he laid a hand on the real Ashlee. He wasn't ready to try, she was his trump card, to be held back for later.

The thin man, Mike had been easy to pacify, but the fat man Stan was definitely, cracking. His time was almost at hand.

The Mend

After Stan found a replacement for the boy's father, Oni intended to see to it that he had his inevitable heart attack.

One less loose string. It would have to be soon.

Noah physically stopped himself from speaking up by biting the inside of his lower lip when his superior officer flashed a photo of Zack and Eric Rubin. Now it was bleeding and his sleeve had a blood mark on it where he had impulsively wiped his mouth on it.

They were saying Zack may have planted a bomb and he and the bomb must be found before he could detonate it. Noah wanted to defend him, to say that they had the wrong guy. He knew it wasn't true. It was definitely not Zack's style to bomb anything. Zack would do something imaginative and harmless to people, like use the building's own security system against itself. He would hack an army helicopter with a virus spreading wi-fi program and fly it over the compound to shut the whole thing down.

Whatever he might do would be spectacular, harmless to life, and meticulously planned. Noah wanted to laugh out loud at the idea of a simple bomb, but then he wondered how The Mend had gotten the photo.

He had taken that particular photo on Eric's ancient film camera at a picnic the day they had graduated High School.

Eric had developed it himself in his basement darkroom. It had never been posted online. There was only one copy. If they had it, it meant they had been inside Zack and Eric's house.

Noah's loyalty was unexpectedly divided. (and he suddenly had the overwhelming urge to go to the bathroom.) He ducked out of the room, pointing to his bloody lip as a reason to get a tissue and just on the other side of the door noticed that his shoelace was loose. He dropped to fix it just as two men with red badges walked by him headed for the room he had just left.

He had not been trained to betray a friend, just the opposite. For the past weeks, he had been training hard in the virtual reality rooms, and except for the fifteen minutes the day before, that the lesson had glitched out and gone offline, he had not missed a session.

Each session started with a flashing graphic: white words on a green background. "Your only mission: Defend The Mend." It had excited him and psyched him up for the game, now it meant nothing.

In the beginning, the games had been mostly about picking out an intruder in the crowd and safely getting them into positions where the Redmen could surround them.

Today the game was about finding an escape route and getting his friends to safety. Now it felt like he was part of the game; as he walked to the bathroom he looked for open doors, windows he could fit through and places to hide.

He remembered one day on their last Spring break when Mr. Rubin had relaxed his strict screen policy and he and Zack had played Berserker Void for 6 hours straight. He had imagined enemies in his peripheral vision all the way home that night and had seen them in his dreams. He was now imagining that the men who had just passed him were coming back for him. As if he was a character in the game, he turned the corner and ducked behind some housekeeping supplies.

He was surprised when the two men did indeed walk quickly by looking in each empty room. He almost called out to them to find out what was going on but the urge to pee became overwhelming.

His bladder and his intestines felt like they would explode, so he ran to the nearest stall and sat down. He subconsciously lifted his feet and put them behind the slightly open door as he relieved himself and even after he was finished, he kept them in place behind the door. He heard the two men whispering to each other as they quickly peeked into the seemingly empty bathroom.

He held his breath until he was sure they were gone, glad that he had not had time to fully close the stall door. It had given them the illusion that the stall was empty.

Chills ran down his spine. They really were after him!

I soft voice whispered, "Noah, can you hear me?" If he had not been still holding his breath he might not have heard the tiny voice that seemed to be coming from a dead white moth on the floor. "Pick up the bug but don't hold the wings."

Noah picked it up; he had always loved creepy-crawlies and remembered helping Zack with a science fair project in which they had remotely controlled a hissing cockroach.

"Can you hear me?" The voice was Zack's and it was stronger.

"Zack, they are looking for you." He whispered, hoping his voice had been loud enough for Zack to hear, but not the Redmen.

"I know Noah, and they're now looking for *you*. Listen to what I'm about to say and follow my directions carefully. I am going to get you out of the building!"

Noah was quietly searching for the speaker that must be hidden in the bug.

"It's the wings, the vibrations are using the wings as a speaker. Hold it up to the light to charge the solar strings on it. RYT!"

He held the bug up to the window and heard a little crunch as he accidentally broke a piece of one dried wing. "RYT" meant "Remember Your Training!" was from today's training session. The glitch wasn't a glitch! It was Zack, reprogramming the game! Noah hesitated for a moment.

His first week of intensive daily programming was telling him to call out to the Redmen, in order to protect The Mend, but his fear of them now overrode his programming and he listened to his friend instead.

He mentally retraced his steps backward from the bathroom to the briefing room and from there to the front door: the only one that remained unlocked during the day. He was surprised to find he remembered every camera, every door and every window.

"Can you still hear me?" The words were fainter but he could still hear. "Mess up your hair and slick it back, use some hand-soap to hold it back. Stuff some little balls of toilet paper against your upper molars, in your cheeks and in your nose; tuck it up so it can't be seen. It will fool the facial recognition software and the people that are looking for you. Leave your jacket there, roll up your sleeves and ditch your badge."

Noah did as he was told and backed out of the bathroom as if he too was looking for the wayward recruit. He saw two other young men in brown shirts about to enter the bathroom. He put on a determined face and barked, "Clear!"

The two recruits closest to him merely glanced into the bathroom and turned to leave. He went in the opposite direction before they got a chance to wonder why he wasn't in regulation uniform.

He expertly zigged and zagged in and out of hallways and hiding spots until he got to the front door where a large group of people, and *Jennifer* was exiting the theater.

"Noah!" she smiled. "I've been looking for you. What happened to your face?"

A Redman he had not previously seen was suddenly coming toward him fast and he had no choice but to run for the front door, hoping to outrun the man and make it to the front gate of the complex before it was closed.

"Give her the bug, grab her badge and RUN!" Noah did. Jennifer screeched and jumped back, nearly dropping the insect and bumping hard into the running Redman who came from nowhere on her left side.

Her mind moved quickly, Noah knew she was afraid of bugs and would never hand her one if it wasn't a.) dead and b.) important. She slipped it into her pocket.

Noah had the momentary break he was looking for as the front door magically opened just as he got to it. A pretty girl in a wheelchair carrying a large bag had hit the automatic door opener and was about to come through. He slipped by her, gave her a quick smile and ran down the front stairs skipping two steps at a time along the way.

The man chasing him was slowed by the girl who wheeled herself diagonally across the doorway to slow the man who seemed to be chasing the cute boy who smiled at her.
He knocked her bag from her hands as he tried to jump through the small space left between her wheelchair and the door. His foot caught on the handle and he fell on his face. It gave Noah even more time. He nearly got across the circular drive that led to the gate when a white security car pulled to an abrupt stop between him and safety.

He stopped and held his hands above his head, defeated.

The back door opened and a small female officer violently pulled him inside. He didn't have the energy to fight. He lay against the seat breathing heavily and wondering why he had not been frisked and cuffed as all suspects had been in training. His head was swimming, he couldn't figure out why all of this was happening.

"Breathe." The driver said. "You're safe now, dork."

"*Zack!* You're driving!" Noah was relieved, stunned and suddenly had to go to the bathroom again.

"The Mend has some pretty great tactical driving software. I found it when I was uploading the program to get you out."

"Why didn't you just program it to make me leave then? How did you get that bug into that bathroom? Hey! Did you program my bodily functions?"

"If you left in the middle of the lesson they would have stopped you. I had to get you someplace private first, it was all I could think of. The most private place in Berserker Void was the police station bathroom, remember?"

"I knew those intensive hours would pay off one day. What about the bug?" Noah had questions about how Zack had programmed his bladder, but they could wait.

"I have so many bugs in there; one of them was bound to look for water. I just had to locate the right one. Hey Noah, there are so many things you need to know. We have to talk, but we have to get away from here first," He spotted a helicopter rising from the pad on the building behind him and stepped on the gas.

They parked the car in a nearby freestanding hotel parking garage. Ada slipped out of the security uniform to reveal a black dress she was wearing underneath and quickly left in an old gray minivan that was waiting. (She was soon stopped and the van was searched by local police as a 'suspicious vehicle' less than two miles away.)

The boys hid in the ventilation duct of the stairwell, out of camera sight and stayed silent as a group of Redmen tracked, searched and retrieved their stolen security car.

Zack disassembled and disabled the tracking and listening devices in the badge Noah had brought while he explained to Noah about his father's apparent overdose.

"He passed peacefully at your house instead of painfully in a hospital, as he probably would have, if his disease had progressed. It was maybe better that way."

He didn't tell him about Jennifer's mother and the Mend's possible role in both deaths. They watched a team of Redmen search every vehicle in the lot. They glanced at the ventilation panel the boys had squeezed through, but apparently judged it too small to fit them.

The Redmen followed every car that entered and left the garage for hours and eventually gave up and went back to the compound.

At Zack's signal, Patrick arrived in another car to retrieve them and they returned to the RV to try to sleep before the next day's ceremony and the biggest part of their plan.

The day was anticipated by everyone but Noah, who didn't understand the intricacies of the plan and chose to stay behind in case they needed someone on the outside. He also needed time alone to grieve his father.

In the early morning hours, he dreamed that he was 10 and his Dad was waking him far too early to take him fishing. When he was nudged awake later, he felt sad that in his dream, he had told him no.

Daybreak just meant more light to Zack. He had spent the night grilling Noah on the location of everything he could remember and filling in holes in his sketch of the complex. He was delighted by how much Noah was able to help. The Mend's security programming was powerful. He remembered every detail he had seen.

Zack held his sketch up to the computer's aerial shot he had found on the internet and saw that he had sketched out most of it. He knew that in those places where Noah had not been, the ones that were not listed in the permits of the building were where he would find Jennifer, his dad…and his father.

Kelsea and Jarrod spent a lot of the night coordinating equipment and timing her separate plan. They had fallen asleep at 3:00.

Ada and Patrick reviewed the plan and fell asleep soon after.

While Noah snored in a sleeping bag on the floor, Zack dressed in a suit, tied his blue tie and combed his hair. When he finished, he nudged Noah with his toe.

"Hey bro, we are leaving in a few minutes, I thought I'd give you a heads up."

"Bring 'em both back, Zack."

"I intend to. Go back to sleep, we will call if we need you. Don't leave the RV, if all goes well, we will be back in about an hour."

Chapter Twenty

"To succeed in your mission, you must have
single-minded devotion to your goal."
-A. P. J. Abdul Kalam

No one said a word on the way to the compound.
Jarrod, also dressed in a suit and tie, drove at exactly
the speed limit.
Ada and Patrick followed in a rental car, if all went
well, they would need the extra seats.

The parking lot was full and attendants waved
them to additional parking in a side lot. Jarrod and
Patrick parked side by side. Ada got out of the car and
into the driver's seat vacated by Jarrod. Kelsea put on
her backpack and a big hoodie with a florist's
delivery service logo on it. She was recognizable and
still had a restraining order against her so she would
not be going in the front door. She picked up a huge
bouquet and headed for the delivery entrance. Ada
and Patrick would wait for their cues to move. They
would need at least one car in motion to escape if
things went wrong.
Kelsea stopped, adjusted her nearly invisible earpiece
and spoke.
"Who hears me?

Each member of the party held up a hand. Everyone went through the same process and when all audio equipment was verified, the three men joined the hundreds of people heading to the front doors of the cathedral-like conference hall.

Everyone passing the gates submitted to a weapon and phone check and all of the men passed through easily. Kelsea's make-up job on Zack's face seemed, so far, to trick the facial recognition software.

They separated, each wandering casually from door to door, leaning and stretching and appearing at each, as if they were waiting for someone.
In actuality they were removing from the hems of their clothing and carefully placing, needle-sized smoke generators above each entrance. Each tiny tube contained two conflicting chemicals with a slowly dissolving barrier between them. The chemicals would react and spread to vaporize the paint and dust that collected above each entrance setting off the smoke detectors.

In every electrical outlet, they slipped tiny micro boosters; programmable remote-control devices Zack had been working on since he was 10 years old.

Zack's early childhood imagination brought shadows to life as monsters. He could battle them in video games, but in the quiet dark of insomniac solitude, the faces of conquered enemies filled his head.

Eric bought motion detector nightlights for every room, which gave Zack an idea for an invisible relay system. He developed a voice-activated remote system to turn on the lights of rooms before he entered at night. He coded it with a password made of consonants that only he could pronounce, to keep people from accidentally turning it on and giving away his embarrassing secret.

He eventually overcame his nyctophobia by playing real life games with Jennifer. They spent after-school hours blindfolding each other and walking through his home by day until they knew each wall by feel and each corner by the number of steps it took to get there. It was her favorite game. They would start from his room and see who could be first to pour a glass of chocolate milk without spilling.

At first, they were evenly matched. But Jennifer was athletic and could walk silently. Zack was fast, but sometimes he would reach the refrigerator to find her standing there with two glasses, one for each of them, still blindfolded.

Sometimes he still used the remotes for convenience when his hands were full and he was glad he had remembered to remove them and put them in his bag before he left home.

The reminder of home made him think of his father. He had to find him and get him out or he would be drowned in The Wash. What was he thinking, signing up to be Mended? Had he himself given him the idea?

He placed the last device by pretending to straighten the seam on his pants and when he stood up, in front of him and on both sides, standing very close, were three large men wearing one red button near the collars of their shirts. He pretended to trip so he could signal his team, "I'M O.K.!"

He saw Patrick and Jarrod, both with panicked looks on their faces start to move toward him but the warning look he sent them stopped them in their tracks before they were detected.

They had all agreed to stick to the plan and they had more important work to do.

The music began in the auditorium and they went in to be seated in the visitor section to continue with the rest of the plan. They accepted blank yellow badges from the brown-shirted youths acting as ushers at the door and scribbled generic names on them.

To his surprise, Zack was not ushered to a secret interrogation room or to his death, but to the front row of the auditorium where he was seated in the middle, directly in front of the orchestra pit. He could see that it was empty but for a few armed Redmen who stared up at him.

"If you get out of line, down you go." Mike said as he sat down beside him, "Enjoy the show."

The music was starting to fade and the signature wavering tone that drew veteran attendees' full attention began.

The drumbeat started and the crowd took their seats chanting. "O-ni! O-ni! O-ni!"

Thomas descended on his platform with his head down and is arms held slightly out from his sides, as if he was too exhausted to initiate the usual embrace.

As the platform met the floor and became steady he lifted his arms in his trademark welcoming gesture. His eyes were fixed on Zack.

"We have so many interesting people with us today. I'd like to welcome all of you, some who have come from such exotic lands as Brazil."

He waved to the right side of the audience and there was concentrated applause from a contingent of Brazilian visitors.

"Germany." He waved to the left and a hearty but controlled applause erupted from a group there.

"And Cleveland." He pointed with one finger to Zack and the whole audience laughed.

"You laugh, but there are some truly talented people from Cleveland. Allow me introduce you to one of them now. This is one of our newest members, Jennifer Wilson. She will be our accompanist today."

Jennifer was seated at the piano. Zack knew that the lights shining in her eyes would not allow her to see that he was there. She had the bug pinned to her collar as he had requested the night before. He wasn't sure the solar string would sustain it as the only bright light in the room was on Oni.

The spotlight blinked off, and new soft lavender light faded on above Jennifer's head. She began to play The Flower Duet.
Zack was calmed by his favorite composition until the thin man tapped him with his elbow.

"You see that lighting harness above her head?" A green laser pointer in his right hand homed in on a heavy, lightly-swaying black metal apparatus.

Zack acted like he was scratching the back of his head and turned on the microphone in his earpiece. "The lights above Jennifer's head?

"Yes. That harness weighs 700 pounds. If I give a signal, that comes down on her. She won't survive that. The only two people who can cause me to give that signal are you, if you try anything and Mr. Oni if he asks properly."

Zack remained quiet and tried to concentrate on the music.

Jennifer finished her performance and sat awaiting her next cue as the light faded back to Oni. He had positioned himself far from the piano.

"Today I'd like to talk to you about the importance of letting go of addictions. There are things in our lives that we cling to. Alcohol. Drugs. Sex. Possessions. Power. All of these things that make us feel good, can kill us…. ANYTHING to which we cling too tightly can jeopardize our future, and the futures of the people we care about most." Thomas turned his eyes to Zack.

"LET GO!" He suddenly shouted the words while staring at Zack's face. Zack didn't take his eyes off of Jennifer but drew a quick silent breath, suppressing a cringe in his seat. Something about Oni's posture told him he wasn't ready to end the game.

Jennifer didn't flinch. Zack waited a moment then looked defiantly at Oni, who was smiling mockingly as if he had gained the upper hand.

"*They* have not learned to let go." He motioned to ten people who were now either walking or being rolled onto stage.

"We have a record number of Mends on our list today for one reason. Addiction! Each of these people has been disabled by (he held his hand over each Provisees head as he named their vice,) a drunk driving accident, an overdose, cirrhosis of the liver, an attempted suicide… because of what they cling to. Their families might have ALLOWED it to happen because sometimes it's easier to live with an addict than to go through the hell of fighting the disease every day. They came to the Mend begging for help because they didn't know where else to turn. Sometimes there IS nowhere to turn. Sometimes you just have to LET GO of your pride and ask for help!"

The audience again applauded. Again, Zack didn't flinch.

"LET GO of your dependence on chemicals."

"LET GO of your lust."

"LET GO of your escape fantasy! LIVE! LIVE! LIVE!"

He raised his arms instructively and immediately the audience was on their feet. The applause lasted several seconds.

He released them from standing by lowering his arms and his head.

"The first man we release from the grip of addiction today also comes from Cleveland. His son brought him here. You will see from the bruises and cuts on his face that he is an old-time brawler." A blanket was pulled back from one of the men in wheelchairs and Eric's battered semi-conscious face appeared on a screen where Zack and the audience could see it, but Jennifer could not.

"Dad!" Zack's exclamation was hidden in the collective gasp of the audience. He controlled his face out of fear that his emotion would bring the lighting down on his best friend.

"Alcoholism nearly killed him. Alcohol is a very hard drug to live with and harder drug to quit. Although we have tried many gentle detox methods, this man has been catatonic for days."

"Help him, God!" a woman called out from the audience.

"WE are going to help this man, by washing away his addiction, washing away his past, washing away his pain."

As he spoke Eric was wheeled out from behind Jennifer, the blanket over most of his head again obscured his face from her view.

The blanket was pulled back as soon as his back was to her just enough to better show the audience two fresh black eyes and a swollen and bloody lip. Zack still did not react.

"Aren't you the object of self-control." The thin man said.

"This man's life is all but over, he needs US to restore him, he needs all of us to send as much good energy as we can, to bring this man back from the edge of death; to heal him, to MEND him."

"Hallelujah." The same woman yelled.

"HalleluYOU, and all of us. Join with me in intention, as I take him into the healing water and wash away his old life."

Thomas backed into the water, and as he put his hands over Eric's hands to pull him into the water, he covertly injected him with a small hypodermic syringe he had palmed. It contained an antidote to the sedative he had been given, so that as he reached the water, he woke up. Thomas wanted Zack to see his suffering, and he wanted Eric to know he was dying.

Thomas was looking forward to this struggle. The audience gasped again as the seemingly magic water began to work. Oni pulled Eric from the chair before he was fully oriented and pushed him into the churning water clamping his legs around his head.

"Jennifer." Zack whispered loudly. "Get out NOW." He leapt from his seat, and hurtled onto the stage, knocking Oni off balance, and threw his arms around Eric, grateful to hear him take a deep breath.

"RELEASE HIM SON! Let him heal, it's for the best." Oni cried as he shoved Zack back and pushed Eric again into the water.

Zack could see his father's replacement being pushed up through a man-sized valve in the plexiglass tube below, by two men in scuba masks. They grabbed his father and pulled him down. Suddenly both of them opened their eyes wide as if surprised. Zack knew they did not expect to see him. His father was yanked down and the massive valve closed behind him. The replacement stood disoriented where he had been.

Zack bellowed in rage. He didn't notice the loud crash as the lights went out on stage. The remotes had finally reached the right system but too late to save his father.

Zack could hear the wheelchair Eric had been in splash into the water as two Redmen stumbled over it on their way to him.

The men pulled Zack off of Oni and hauled him off stage in the near blackness. He shook his earpiece out and heard it plop into the water. He might have been caught, but he would not give away his team.

"Lock the exit gates." Oni barked to a man at the edge of the stage. "This service is not over."

The lights of the theater came on again and began flashing red as the back-up generator kicked in, and the fire alarm sounded as the smoke generators were also began doing their job. People flowed out of the exit doors. No one noticed that the lighting apparatus had flattened the piano stool where Jennifer had been sitting.

Jennifer was nowhere to be seen. She had gotten the message.

"You killed my dad." Zack's voice was steady, which surprised him, considering he was being held off the ground by two giant henchmen.

He was overwhelmed by their brutal grasps as they drug him down a hallway, a set of stairs and through two doors. He was relieved when they finally threw him onto a chair. By then his mind had gone blank and his body numb. For all his intelligence, he could not fathom life without Eric. It had never occurred to him that he might have to.

"You killed my dad." He said again, staring at Oni with more restraint than he thought he could muster. "You killed him, that was a mistake."

"We both know I AM your dad, you inchworm."

Only Mike and Zack stood before him now but Thomas could account for the other two, he had told Forrester to dispatch the fat man that morning. Forrester always did as he was told. Stan was dead and Forrester would be bringing the girl along at any moment.

"Zack Rubin... Your name is really Zack Walters and you're an aberration. You're only here because I fucked my sister, did you know that?" He could see by the unflinching gaze of the kid that he already knew.

"If you think about it, we're not that different. I fucked her, but you killed her. We were both in that hole." He laughed out loud for biting emphasis but Zack sat motionless.

Oni was getting frustrated; he had to get *some* emotion from the boy; he had to crack him. He stood too close to the seated boy and put his crotch close to his face for humiliation. Zack still didn't move.

Oni's breath was audible as he stood hovering above Zack.

He turned his back to give the kid an opportunity to attack. The thin man was close and several Redmen were standing against a wall to protect him if it happened.

The boy was as still as a gravestone.

"When our friend, Jennifer gets here, I'm going to fuck her too, then I'm going to kill her and that will also… be your fault." The kid still didn't falter. Oni had no way of knowing that all it would have taken to rattle him was one little touch.

"Get him out of here, bring him back when Forrester returns. Meanwhile, program him in the experience chamber. Give him schizophrenia"

"He's really smart Thomas, are you sure that's going to work?" Mike asked. He reached for the boy but stopped when Thomas spoke.

"Are you questioning me?

The Mend

Mike fixed his eyes on the floor.

Thomas hissed. "There are only two kinds of people that can't be programmed by my method: psychopaths and idiots. This kid is neither."

Thomas turned back to the Redman in charge of the group, "When you're done with him. Bring the people back into the theater."

Mike motioned to the door. The boy stood up and went willingly, flanked by Redmen. He wanted to be as far from Oni as he could get. Rage was boiling inside of him and when he was angry, he didn't think clearly. Even in his grief, he had to concentrate on the plan. It had to happen now, or it never would.

Forrester sat in the back-seat of a moving white sedan bandaging Jennifer's wounds. He needed her to be healthy. He was in charge of her and she was important to the plan.
The lighting harness had fallen harder than he had anticipated and a small piece of ivory from the piano had ricocheted into the back of her thigh narrowly missing an artery.

"I hope Zack knows what he's getting into." He said to Kelsea who sat in the front with another kid who looked baffled.
"Oni's not stupid."

"Neither is Zack, trust me." Jennifer interjected.

"But can we trust him?" Forrester asked, "Those programming tactics are seriously powerful. Oni built his entire empire on them."

"Zack can't be programmed, he's like a machine." She answered. "He will *do* the programming."

"That's the plan." Kelsea replied. "We will see."

They drove to the RV where Ada and Patrick were waiting with four more kids. The boy Kelsea had retrieved, completed the forum-posting group. Four of the five had come in together. They were all safe.

Noah appeared in the doorway of the RV carrying Kelsea's loaded gun. He pointed it at Forrester.

"You betrayed Thomas. My only mission: Defend the Mend."

"Noah no!" Jennifer stepped in front of Forrester.

Noah's hands shook and for a moment Jennifer feared his shaking would pull the trigger. The gun fell to the ground. Noah shook his head and blinked.

"Seriously powerful programming." Forrester repeated. Jennifer went to hug her quivering friend.

"We have to go back." Forrester called to her. "Are you ready?"

"Noah and I are all Zack has now, I have to be."

Forrester helped her into the car and drove back to the compound, filling her in on her part of the plan along the way. He parked in the back near the building and punched in his code at the private door. Nothing happened. Good.
He tried again and when the door didn't open, he pressed the intercom.

"Hey, I can't get in, I have an important package for the boss."

A muffled voice from the speaker said, "All the codes have been changed, for the time being it's all optical recognition. I'll have to get Mr. Oni, he has the only clearance for that door. Hold on."

Forrester was glad his code override had worked and hoped calling Thomas to the door would give Zack enough time. The door buzzed and he pulled it open to find Thomas standing behind it. Oni immediately wrapped his arm around Jennifer and pulled her close to him.

"I was worried about you. After all that happened this morning and everyone scattered to the wind, I was afraid you had gotten lost."

"It was terrifying!" Jennifer had discovered she had a third natural skill: acting. "When everyone ran out I followed, but they stopped us from going back in. Mr. Forrester brought me around here to the shortcut."

"Good that he did." Oni smiled a fatherly smile and winked at Forrester. "Good that he did."

"I should probably fill you in on what happened." Forrester said as he stood in place. Every second he could distract Oni counted. "We are still figuring things out, but it seems the fire alarms malfunctioned and somehow caused a lighting short. He turned to Jennifer. "Apparently, it burned a line that was holding up your lighting."

"You know, you're lucky to be alive!" Thomas exclaimed.

"I know! I just got this cut." She lifted her skirt high and showed far more leg than she had to. It got his attention. She held the skirt up a little longer and glanced at Oni's eyes.

His pupils were expanding and his smile was fixed. She was getting to him.

"Let's go to my suite, I want to reunite you with someone I think you know." He ran his hand down her back and hesitated just at the base of her spine before pulling away. He would have his fun with her later.

They followed the maze of dark, hazy hallways, Jennifer held onto Oni to keep her balance, partly because of her injured leg, partly to keep him distracted and partly because she wanted to control where his hands were going.

Forrester walked a pace ahead to guide them through the still smoky halls and when they got to the office he opened the door for them to step inside. Mike and the Redmen where gone.

Thomas opened a box on his desk and flipped a switch.

Zack, looking like Jennifer had never seen him, appeared on a screen, seated in a small black stall the size of a photo booth. He was alone.

His dilated eyes were bloodshot, his shirt was open to his waist and his tie, still on his neck was askew, his arms were behind him. He was rocking chaotically back and forth. The normally quiet and still Zack looked utterly mad.

"Hello son, how are you?"

"Fuck you." Zack spat back. "Don't touch her."

"Oh, I won't just touch her. She and I are going to have fun in a lot of ways."

As Thomas was speaking, Forrester unexpectedly cuffed Jennifer who screamed and tried to run for the door.

Thomas forced her down onto a couch opposite the camera. He pried her mouth open with his fingers and shoved a lemon from a basket of fruit into her mouth then took a moment to stand back and look at her. She was so beautiful.

"You're going to see it all, in fact you're going to feel it too. You see you are in a virtual reality room and those electrodes we stuck in your head are directly connected to pain and pleasure centers in your brain. They are interpreters. If I do this, what do you feel?" He pinched the back of his hand.

"Ouch." Zack flinched and looked at his hand to see if it was turning red. It wasn't.

"But we are going to go a bit further. You see, because you are my son, you and I share a lot of the same genetic material so we probably have the same synapses and low tolerance to pain." He shook his hand to shake off the pain of the pinch.

"That means we have similar preferences in pleasure. I want you to feel everything and you will. I'm all about neuron-programming. I've studied this for years; it's what got me here."

"A few months ago, I developed this." He held up a flexible netting that looked like a metal wig liner. When he put it on, his hair poked through it and stood up in many directions making him look like a mad scientist, which indeed he had become.

"You will feel everything I feel, *and* you will think everything I think. It goes only one way so you get to experience your horror alone."

He put it on his head and suddenly Zack felt a surge in his groin and a giddy, high feeling like he had once during a fever.

Thomas pulled up Jennifer's skirt revealing her clean white panties and looked over his shoulder to see if Zack was watching.

"I'm warning you, don't touch her." He could feel the satisfaction Oni felt at his anger. The conflicting feeling of Oni's inflating ego and his anger made him dizzy. Zack tried to stand up but fell backward in a spin.

Oni was standing close enough and was distracted just long enough for Jennifer to free herself from the purposely loose cuffs and slip one onto Thomas's wrist where she tightened it and quickly grabbed his other arm, cuffing it too, confining him now harmless to the woodwork of the arm of the couch. She jumped out of reach of his wildly swinging legs.

"Forrester stop her!" Oni barked and Zack felt fear and confusion as Forrester walked the opposite direction. Jennifer pulled the lemon out of her mouth and threw it on the floor.

Oni's right-hand man instead went to his desk and flipped another switch in the box revealing to Thomas that he was not actually in his office as he had thought.

He had followed Forrester, distracted by Jennifer and smoke through twisting wrong turns to a virtual reality room that had been set up to look just like his office. Getting him into the programming room was the last uncontrolled variable.

The devices that Kelsea had planted had been easy to find in the computers so that Forrester had his mission and an excuse to schedule a sweep that he would supervise.

It was the perfect opportunity to put projectors, relays and switches exactly where his allies needed them. Another sweep would not be necessary. He had time to set up the perfect situation to show Thomas the error of his ways.

Forrester started to usher Jennifer out of the room but she stopped him. She stripped the netting from Oni's now quiet head and put it on her own. Then she looked directly into the camera that she knew Zack was watching.

Zack's head suddenly filled with a strong wave of love she felt for him and the pride of the moment. There were no conflicting feelings. They both felt the same way.

Forrester left the room and waited for Jennifer as she replaced the net on Thomas's head.

Zack, suddenly calm again, set to work reversing the signal before handing identical devices to Ada and

Patrick who were waiting off camera. They looked at a wall-sized projection of their son, Charlie, in front of Oni. Charlie was laughing up at them from his wheelchair. Before they turned Thomas over to the police, there were things they wanted Oni to feel and do.

Chapter Twenty-One

"Hard times don't create heroes. It is during the hard
times when the 'hero' within us is revealed."
-Bob Riley

Thomas Oni held his head, shoulders and hands low
as his platform descended for the final time.

This time it was more than just a gesture of
humility that he had learned all those years ago on
CDs he memorized in the beat-up stolen car.

As he reached the stage, no music played. The
rumblings of the reorganized crowd grew quiet
organically until the silence in the cavernous meeting
hall was tangible.

"I have a short lesson to finish today." He started
at a whisper. "And I'll get right to it. I'm sorry that
technical difficulties disrupted our service. I
apologize for that."

A few motherly voices called out words of
forgiveness. Others were still whispering of the
experience.

"I have a lot of apologizing to do today. You see, I built The Mend using the research of people much smarter than I am." He looked around the now still audience. This was a very different service. No one knew what was going on. Even he wasn't sure.

"This system, that has saved so many of you from desperation, disease and poverty, is a collection of thoughts from the world's best behaviorists and psychiatrists. But it's not what you think it is." Zack sat back and waited for the confession he had programmed into Oni's brain.

Thomas's eyes stared at the floor in front of him and a new light appeared in his eyes. There would be no confession.

"It's so much more. It's alive because of you and what you bring each week. It has evolved because of YOU!"

The whoops, cheers and applause from the audience energized him as his unexpected words confused Jennifer, Zack and Forester.

"I would like to CONFESS that when I started out I just wanted to be rich and famous. Don't we ALL want to be rich and famous?" The crowd again applauded and life seemed to be trickling back into his mannerisms.

"We ALL want to be more than we are, and we CAN BE. However, there are people here that believe

WE are wrong. They think these methods are too extreme."

He nodded twice and a large group of young men in brown polos started down the aisles. Thomas held up one hand and they stopped, clustering at both ends of the row in which Forrester, Zack and Jennifer sat together.

"They have tried to stop me from helping you, and until this very MOMENT, they thought they had succeeded."

He glared at Forrester, who reached into his shoulder holster to find it was empty. Thomas continued.

"Seventeen years ago, I set up weekly classes, and at first I had just three students. You might know them as the three directors that keep The Mend running all over the world. Two of them are here today. My right-hand man Forrester Campbell..." Thomas motioned to Forrester as his face appeared on the screen above them. There was light applause. He looked confused.

"…and Mike Wagner." The thin man, sitting in the front row was oblivious to what was going on behind him so he smiled and waved as the audience clapped for him as well.

"I took those three first students off the street, healed them of their maladies and gave them everything they have, which is a lot, believe me. Now I feel great sorrow… because today I learned that that they have betrayed me and The Mend and are attempting to stop the good work we do here." The crowd booed.

Mike looked alarmed. He glanced over his shoulder, saw the brown shirts and thought to leap into the orchestra pit but it was still full of Redmen, who were watching on a screen of their own.

Jennifer looked at Zack and Forrester who also seemed puzzled. Oni had been programmed to confess! Something was wrong!

Forrester was suddenly remembering what Oni had said about the two types of people that can't be programmed: idiots and psychopaths. It occurred to him that he understood the latter part of the statement a bit too late.

"I will testify to you more specifically about what these two men have done later, but today is not about justice or retribution, it is about healing, so, they will be leaving us for the rest of the service."

The brown-shirted boys pulled Forrester, Zack and Jennifer from their seats. They didn't protest. They were outnumbered 5 to 1.

Mike also knew better than to protest, but he would not go down without a fight. He attempted to jump the orchestra pit to get to Oni as he had seen the boy do earlier, but he slipped, fell in and was immediately immobilized by Redmen.

Oni went on as if it had not happened. Most of the audience had not seen it.

"I'd like to dedicate today's Wash ceremony to someone who can't be here with us today, someone who believed in the healing message of The Mend, my third and only loyal protégé, Stan Kaufman, who died of a heart attack this morning. On his deathbed he revealed the actions of his traitorous friends. He was innocent. Rest in peace big man."

The familiar music started and Oni pushed a button on the remote control in his hand. The screen flickered, showing an old photo of Stan wearing a suit and tie, he was smiling with one arm around Oni. It was taken when they were breaking ground for the now colossal structure of the cathedral theater. The screen paused on the photo for a moment and then the *very much alive* fat man appeared in front of the screen behind him.

Stan was not smiling and he held a tiny vial which he turned over, the gesture proving its emptiness.

A look of horrible recognition passed over Oni's face. He took a deep breath and glanced up at the half-drunk bottle of water he had left on the platform.

His speech pattern became more urgent as the seated crowd started to stir.

"I had intended to give a new start to The Mend today; to step into the waters of The Wash and to heal my own life as proof to you that this system works. But what you see here shows there is no time for that. This betrayal runs deeper than even I knew.

Thomas moved toward the pool which was now being exposed again by the slowly rolling platform.

"I've given everything I have, everything I own and everything am to The Mend. If my methods have been a bit extreme, it's because I have been deceived into believing I was doing the right thing. I am a victim of my own methods." Oni's eyes seemed to be glancing around looking for a place to run, but his body wasn't moving.

"Friends, I did everything I did to make the world a better place. I did it for humanity, and I will PROVE that it has been twisted into something grotesque by those I trusted most."

He suddenly clutched his chest and stumbled backward, heading offstage toward the door to his bedroom where he kept the antidote to the contents of Stan's empty vial.

The drug that he had entrusted to Forrester, meant for Stan, was beginning to do its work on HIM.

He tripped over an electrical cable and fell backward and was caught in the waiting arms of *Eric Rubin*!

Oni went silent in shock.

"You did it for money and power. There is no healing in the kind of evil you have been preaching." His microphone picked up Eric's strong words and broadcast them to the squealing, mumbling, whispering audience now back on their feet.

Eric lifted Oni back to an upright position and stepped back away from him.
Police officers behind Eric and at every doorway moved into position.

The reality of what they were seeing suddenly occurred to the audience. The man with Thomas Oni had seemed just an hour earlier to be completely mended. Now the years and scars that had been stripped from his face, were back. His busted lip was scabbed over and the black bruises under his eyes were less swollen but darker than before.

Thomas looked off stage and saw police officers at both ends. He looked to the audience and saw more of them coming down the aisles, led by Martin Anderson.

Forrester and Stan held up their hands willingly, they were cuffed and quietly taken into custody.

Mike, now free of the Redmen who were running for the exits, also ran but was met at the door by an army of officers and like the Redmen, was wrestled to the ground and arrested.

Thomas, still clutching his chest, tottered strategically toward the swirling water at center stage. He kicked a hidden switch that manually opened the hatch, took a deep breath, leapt into the water and felt for the switch that he could open in case he fell in during a Wash ceremony.

Normally, a loyal frogman was in the next chamber ready to catch the dead Provisee and push up the replacement. The escape hatch was in there. They used it to get themselves out before they sent the dead Provisee efficiently into the grinder.

He reached for the switch but it had been capped. He felt for the handle of the exit door but it was locked from the outside.

His stomach wrenched as he heard the electric spinning noise that meant the grinder was engaging and the bottom valve was opening. He had one last moment of drowning panic, witnessed only by Charlie's devoted father, Patrick, as he opened the floor hatch and Thomas Oni was pulled feet first into the grinder.

Zack broke free of the baffled brown badges and ran as fast as his legs could carry him to the stage and threw himself into the arms of his father.

"I thought you were dead! How did you get out of The Wash?"

"It was Stan." Eric said. "He couldn't kill a van full of kids. It was too much for him. He went to Forrester to resign. Forrester filled him in and he started working with him. He came back and fitted me with a harness your friend Kelsea designed. He rigged it to the wheelchair to anchor me and met me at the escape door under that pool. The two scuba men that pulled me down were not so lucky."

Zack had not let go of his dad and he still held him close. "Why did you come here?"

"I thought if I got in, I could warn Jennifer and Noah, I didn't know they would accept me! I'm not that sick!"

"But you said cancer... weeks."

"I was telling them it had been a few weeks since my diagnosis I may have exaggerated the severity. I have a very slow-moving, fully operable cancer. I've probably got years...and there is all this new technology."

Jennifer and Noah fought through the tightly-packed crowd being sorted out by the police. They didn't bother with the stairs and leapt onto the stage to wrap their arms around Eric as well.

Kelsea, standing with Ada by Jarrod's side, waved to them as she filled Martin Anderson in on the details. Martin, in cooperation with the LAPD, scored the biggest and last arrests of his career.

Kelsea pointed to the cameras that were still running. He would have years of footage to prove this case. He retired a hero.

Chapter Twenty-Two

"Being fully present is the
best guarantee for a bright future."
- Guy Finley

Forrester would be freed on immunity. His numerically coded journals implicated Walters/Oni and Mike Wagner as responsible for multiple felonies. As he had been the one that installed the cameras and recording equipment, he knew exactly where to stay out of sight and quiet. There was no evidence to implicate him in any crime. He testified against Mike and moved to Boston to spend Saturday mornings eating breakfast with his daughter Ashlee, her new husband and eventually four grandchildren.

In addition to charges of murder, racketeering and rape, Mike was implicated as a serial child molester of several young people in The Mend's youth program. His years in prison were not pleasant.

Stan died of an apparent heart attack before the case went to trial in a hotel in Bakersfield. His body was found by the housekeeping staff.

The responding EMTs would describe that he was sitting, holding an empty glass and an open bottle of 40-

year-old bourbon. The tiny vial was never discovered in his stomach, there was no autopsy.

Zack was the only heir to Oni's empire, which he immediately dismantled to start a foundation for the victims of The Mend. He built a process called JENZ, (Joint Electro-Neuro Zymogen) essentially micro-robots that allow paralyzed people to feel sensation.

Jennifer ran the business side of the company and started The Debra Wilson Scholarship for nursing students.

After college, Noah became the company's legal representation. He found and married the pretty young woman who had helped him escape and she became his legal partner.

The Mend compound sat empty for years as police used DNA from the soil to identify many, but not all of Thomas's victims.

It temporarily became a pharmaceutical factory, now it is empty.

The flowers that grew in the gardens still thrive among the green weeds as memorial spots of yellow, blue, purple, orange and red in the wild lot behind it.

No one goes there to enjoy them.

Epilogue:

Anita erased her employee file from the computers of The Mend and downloaded its database into her phone. It was one of just a few valuable things she collected from her swift, quiet exit of The Mend.

She missed Thomas's generosity, but she had been paid well, had invested enough to start a new life and so far, it had been glorious.

She looked up at the red campaign banners rippling in the flow of the air conditioner above her then waved good night to the volunteer that was locking up. He looked sharp in a new charcoal gray polo. She would have to remember to collect the old brown ones from all the "new" volunteers she recruited. She could thank Thomas for them as well.

She clicked the call button of the first number on the screen and listened as it went straight to voicemail, as she hoped it would.

"Hi, it's Anita," she sang into the headset. "I'm calling a very *exclusive* list of people in hopes of your generosity to my newly launched campaign for Congress. I just saw your new movie. It's spectacular.

Speaking of movies, I'm sending you a clip of one of my own. I think you'll find it fascinating. I'll be in touch."

On the screen, 15-year-old Jackie was nervously removing her new blue shirt in front of a fully-naked, fully-aroused, very recognizable actor. Anita clicked "send" and went to the next video.

It featured a politician and a pretty 14-year-old boy named Vince. She clicked on the next phone number on the screen.

She was confident in her chances of being elected.